Knight of Betrayal

A Yorkshire Ghost Story

by

Karen Perkins

LionheART Publishing House

First published in Great Britain in 2015 by
LionheART Publishing House

Copyright © Karen Perkins 2015,2021

ISBN: 978-1-910115-34-3

LionheART Publishing House
Harrogate
UK

lionheartpublishinghouse@gmail.com

Cover Design by CC Morgan Creative Visuals

Cast List

Main Historical Figures and Titles

Henry II – King of England, Duke of Normandy, Duke of
Aquitaine, Lord of Ireland
Thomas Becket – Archbishop of Canterbury

Sir Hugh de Morville – Baron of Burgh-on-the-Sands, Lord of
the Manor of Cnaresburg
Sir William de Tracy – Baron of Bradninch
Sir Reginald FitzUrse – Lord of the Manor of Williton
Sir Richard le Brett (also known as Richard le Breton/de Brito)

Cnaresburg and Yorkshire:

Sir William de Percy – Baron of Topcliffe, Lord of Spofford and
Wetherby
Sir William de Courcy – Lord of Harewood
Sir William de Stoteville
Lady Helwise de Morville

Other:

Sir Hamelin Plantagenet – Earl of Surrey
Sir William de Mandeville – Earl of Essex
Sir Richard de Humez – Constable of Normandy
Sir Ranulf de Broc – Overlord of Saltwood Castle
Hugh Mauclerk

Modern Characters

Helen Forrester – director and scriptwriter
Paul Fuller – plays Henry II
Charlie Thorogood – plays Thomas Becket
Ed Thomas – plays Hugh de Morville
Mike Bates– plays William de Tracy
Dan Stoddard – plays Reginald FitzUrse
Sarah Stoddard – plays Richard le Brett
Alec Greene – sound and lighting technician
Donna – owner of Spellbound
John Stoddard – son of Dan and Sarah
Kate Stoddard – daughter of Dan and Sarah
Richard Armitage – feva committee member

Place Names

I have used the historical spellings of place names in the knights'
timeline and modern ones in the Castle Players' timeline:

Cnaresburg – Knaresborough
Goldesburgh – Goldsborough
Plumton – Plompton
Riche Mont – Richmond
River Nydde – River Nidd
Screven – Scriven
Spofford – Spofforth

Chapter 1

Saltwood Castle

29th December 1170

'This is our chance. You heard the King's words,' Sir Reginald FitzUrse said. 'Becket has shamed him.'

'He called us all drones and traitors for allowing Becket to get away with it,' Sir William de Tracy said.

'Yes!' shouted FitzUrse, and slammed his fist against the table to emphasise the word. The four men sitting with him flinched at his exuberance. Sir Reginald FitzUrse, or The Bear as he liked to be called, resembled the ursine creatures he was named for in more ways than one. Large, hairy, loud and strong with a temper to beware of, his friends and vassals were afraid of him, although were eager to please him – even the mature yet impressionable Sir William de Tracy. Sir Hugh de Morville exchanged an exasperated glance with Sir Ranulf de Broc – the overlord of Saltwood Castle and the knights' host.

'No one has avenged me,' FitzUrse quoted their king, Henry Plantagenet of England, leaning forward now and staring at each man in turn. 'No one has avenged me,' he repeated.

'A clear plea,' Broc, FitzUrse's master in the King's household, agreed. 'King Henry raised Thomas Becket from a low-born clerk to Archbishop of Canterbury, for God's sake, and look how he has repaid him.'

1

Tracy nodded with enthusiasm. 'Yes! He excommunicated l'Évêque, Foliot and Salisbury, and for no good reason.'

Broc glanced at him in annoyance. 'As I was saying, two bishops and the Archbishop of York excommunicated and damned for eternity for crowning the Young King.'

'Well, his father, King Henry, still lives.' Morville tried to calm the rising tempers as Broc signalled to his steward to refill the jugs of fine Rhenish wine. 'It may be customary for a king to crown his successor before his own death in Normandy, but it is rare in England. Only King Stephen did it, and that was just to spite the Empress Matilda.'

'It is King Henry's prerogative!' FitzUrse slammed the table again, and Sir Richard le Brett – still a boy – steadied the now full flagon of Rhenish, then proceeded to empty it into goblets. Morville sighed as he watched Tracy down half in a single gulp.

'Yes,' Tracy slurred. 'It's nothing to do with Becket. It would not surprise me if Becket meant to depose the Young King and try for the crown himself.'

'Always was an ambitious bastard,' Brett agreed, then picked up a bone and noisily sucked the marrow from it.

'Are you sure we arrived on England's shores before Mandeville and Humez?'

'Yes, I have had my men patrolling the coasts to slow them down. They failed me when they allowed Becket to beach from France. They will not fail me again.'

'How can you be so sure?' FitzUrse asked, pointing a half-eaten pheasant leg at his host.

Broc laughed. 'Oh, I can be sure. One captain lost his head – the rest all want to keep theirs.'

Morville drained his wine, once again regretting FitzUrse's choice of ally. The other men laughed, and Morville realised they were well into their cups. He poured more wine and drank again – in their cups may well be the only way they'd survive this day.

'So we shall beat them to Becket?' Tracy asked.

'We have to,' Broc said. 'If they arrest Becket, they shall receive all the accolades – the two of them already hold more castles and titles than the five of us put together. If we can take Becket to the King, he will surely be indebted to us and who knows what his favour may bring?'

'Then what are we waiting for?' FitzUrse roared, pushing himself to his feet. His fellow knights followed suit, throwing down the remains of the meat they'd been gnawing on and draining their goblets.

The men-at-arms seated in the hall below shoved as much meat in their mouths as possible before following their masters to the stables. Half an hour later the company of over a hundred armed men cantered through the imposing towers of the castle's gate and took the road to Canterbury.

While Broc garrisoned his men in the town, FitzUrse, Morville, Tracy and Brett – along with a small retinue of their most trusted vassals – clattered through the gatehouse to the Archbishop's Palace and dismounted in the courtyard.

Morville glanced at his companions, still concerned at the glazed eyes which the three-hour ride had done nothing to clear.

FitzUrse produced another wineskin which he passed to Tracy after taking a large slug himself. 'Are you ready for this?'

'We need to disarm,' Morville said before the other knights – still focused on the wine – could reply.

'Disarm? God's blood, Hugh, we are here on the King's business.'

'This is a house of God – the Archbishop will have mere monks, priests and clerks about him. No men-at-arms and no weapons. We shall not need arms to arrest him.'

'He is correct,' said Brett, 'we can kill him with our bare hands if necessary.'

'Richard!' Morville was horrified. 'We are not here to kill him, merely to arrest him and take him to King Henry to deal with as *he* sees fit.'

'If necessary, the boy said. If necessary,' FitzUrse jumped to his sycophant's defence.

'Why should it be necessary?' Morville asked.

'Thomas Becket stands against not only the Young King, but King Henry himself. He has just returned from exile. Look what he has done already, who knows what he would do when called to account? We must be ready for anything.'

'But we leave swords and mail here,' Morville insisted. Despite FitzUrse's bluster, as Baron of Burgh-on-the-Sands, Sir Hugh de Morville held the highest status amongst the four men.

FitzUrse hesitated, then succumbed to him. 'Very well, if it shall make you happy. Arms and mail stay here.'

Mauclerk, Morville's clerk, helped the knights out of their heavy hauberks and mail hoods and piled the armour, along with their long blades, under a nearby mulberry tree. 'They will be safe here with me,' he said.

FitzUrse glanced round the knights. William de Tracy in particular looked nervous and vulnerable without his arms or armour. Despite his thirty seven years and own barony, he appeared younger with a boyish clean-shaven face, copper curls and slim build. At this moment, if one ignored the lines of worry around his eyes, he appeared a child.

FitzUrse passed him the wine. 'Who are we?' he called.

'The King's men,' the other three chorused.

'Who are we?' FitzUrse shouted louder.

'The King's men!'

'WHO ARE WE?' Louder still.

'THE KING'S MEN!'

'Á Henry Plantagenet!' FitzUrse roared, and the others joined in, the wineskin forgotten and trampled on the cobblestones.

FitzUrse crossed to the door of the great hall and banged his clenched paw upon it. 'In the name of the King, open up!' Then again, and again, the other knights joining in the cry and the thumps on the door – even Morville was carried away now with the purpose of their mission.

'Thomas Becket, in the name of King Henry, permit entry or we shall break down this door!' Tracy yelled, then stumbled back at the sound of bolts being drawn.

Chapter 2

'This is an insult,' FitzUrse fumed. 'He affronts the King by keeping us waiting.'

'I suspect it is the four of us he intends to disrespect,' Morville countered.

FitzUrse glared at him. 'We are the King's men. He affronts us, he affronts King Henry.'

The entrance of a monk interrupted the resultant awkward silence. 'The Archbishop shall see you now.' He backed against the open door as the knights passed through.

Thomas Becket was still seated at table in the company of near half a dozen men, and Morville recognised John de Salisbury, Benedict de Peterborough and William de Canterbury. A monk seated at Becket's right hand glared at them, but the knights dismissed him. He was of no consequence.

'Ahh, Hugh, Reginald, William, how good of you to welcome me back to England's fine shores. It has been long that I have been away, and there is no sweeter pleasure than returning home and reuniting with old friends.'

The knights faltered, unsure of how to proceed in the face of this effusive and seemingly sincere welcome. Then FitzUrse stepped forward.

'We are not here to welcome you, Becket.' The Archbishop's brows rose at this calculated insult; the proper form of address was Your Grace. 'We are here to return you to Normandy. You have grievously wronged the King.'

'Wronged the King? My Lord, what do you mean? What evil and disgusting lies have been told of me?'

'No lies, Becket.' FitzUrse's face reddened further under the mass of hair that covered it. 'Do you deny that you have excommunicated three loyal subjects of King Henry? Roger de Pont l'Évêque, Gilbert Foliot and Jocelin de Salisbury – the King's most loyal Archbishop of York and two of his most loyal bishops. What say you to the charge?'

'Those facts are correct. Pray, what is your complaint?'

'What is my complaint?' FitzUrse's voice rose and he stepped forward, then glanced back at his fellow knights who stayed where they were and showed no sign of speaking. He grunted in exasperation.

'Those three honourable, devout and loyal subjects met the King's wishes in crowning his son, Henry the Young King, as his successor. As you know this is normal practice in France and a custom that our king desired to be enacted on England's shores. Yet you bring down the worst punishment on these good, God-fearing men – a punishment worse even than torture and death, for it will condemn their souls to reside in Hell for eternity.' FitzUrse paused for breath, and Archbishop Becket waved him to continue with a smile. He looked as relaxed as if he were enjoying a much anticipated reunion with the friends he had claimed them to be.

FitzUrse continued with another aggravated glance at his silent companions, 'By excommunicating them for the crowning of the Young King, you have declared yourself against not only the Young King, but King Henry himself.' FitzUrse pushed himself to his tallest and thrust out his chest. 'As such, by the command of King Henry, I arrest you for the good of England, and charge you with sedition and treason.'

'Sedition *and* treason? Surely it must be one or the other, Reginald. Committing treason or inciting others to commit treason. King Henry would know that you cannot charge me with both. Which tells me that you and your friends are here on your own recognisance, perhaps to find favour with Henry, hmm?' Becket stood as he spoke and planted his fists on the table before him, pulling the full force of his position as Archbishop of Canterbury about him. FitzUrse stood his ground, but the others shrank back.

'Henry also knows that it is the duty of the Archbishop of Canterbury to crown a king, an obligation not given to the Archbishop of York nor any other man. King Henry accuses you as traitor. You shall come with us.'

'Do I need to remind you that you are my sworn vassal, Reginald? Your good self, Hugh de Morville, and you, William de Tracy, all swore fealty to me. You,' he peered at Brett, 'you have not, although I know you, do I not?'

Brett ground his teeth, but said naught.

'No matter. As my sworn vassals, I demand you leave my presence. I shall hear no more of this nonsense.'

FitzUrse strode forward to Becket's table and planted his own fists upon it. 'Yes, we swore fealty to you, but as Chancellor of England, not as Archbishop of Canterbury. Yet even so, the fealty sworn was second to King Henry. I – we—' he glanced behind him, disgusted that his fellow knights still hung back, '— serve the King above all others. Including you.'

'Then tell Henry I have no issue with either himself or the Young King. Coronations in England are performed by the Archbishop of Canterbury and no other. Now leave my presence and explain to *our* king that I am his loyal servant still. The excommunications stand and are an issue between myself, the bishops concerned, Pope Alexander III, and no other. King Henry has my love and fealty, as he has yours. Please try your best to understand that and depart. This has grown tiresome. I bid you goodnight, My Lords.'

Becket turned, his green robes swirling, and left by a door the knights had not noticed, followed by his clerics. At a loss and alone in the great hall, the four knights turned to depart.

Chapter 3

'Where is he?' Broc – standing at the head of a column of men-at-arms – demanded. The knights looked at each other and said naught. 'Are you telling me that four knights of the realm, four of the King's own warriors, were no match for one paltry churchman?'

FitzUrse stepped forward. 'We offered Becket a chance to come gracefully. He refused. Now we shall take him.'

Broc glanced at the pile of swords and mail with contempt. 'You had better dress yourselves then.'

The knights hurried to the mulberry tree and Brett hauled up the first heavy hauberk: FitzUrse's. He held the coat of mail wide, heaved it up, and dropped it over FitzUrse's outstretched arms and shoulders. The Bear grunted as the weight landed on him, then straightened up and shrugged it over his torso. Mauclerk did the same for Morville, then Tracy and Brett helped each other into theirs.

'Ready boys?' Broc taunted.

'Always, My Lord,' FitzUrse replied, hefting his sword, then strode back to the door of the great hall of the Archbishop's Palace. It remained barred to them.

Tracy glanced behind at the smirking Broc, and called, 'Round the back! There must be another way in.'

Without a word – or a glance at his master – FitzUrse led the way round the great building to the administration buildings attached to the north side of the cathedral.

'There.' Tracy pointed at a window under repair. 'The masons have left it incomplete!'

'Up you go then, William,' FitzUrse said. 'Climb in and unlock the door.'

Tracy glanced at him, then back at the window. His fear of FitzUrse was greater than his fear of heights, however, and he searched the stonework for a path up to the open invitation.

Just as he was about to start his climb, Brett called, 'One moment, William.'

Tracy turned and smiled when he saw the young knight dragging a ladder.

'The masons must have thrown it into the shrubbery and fled when they saw the men.' Brett nodded at the score of men-at-arms behind Broc.

'Your lucky day,' Broc said. 'What are you waiting for?'

Tracy glanced at him, then led the way up to the window, followed by Brett. Morville was the only man to think to hold the ladder steady for them.

When both had disappeared through the narrow aperture into the archive building, then made their way downstairs to let the others in, FitzUrse led the way to the chancel door to gain entrance to the cathedral itself, sword drawn.

'It's locked,' Tracy said.

'Then we'll break it down,' FitzUrse said. He raised his hand to bang for entry but the door swung away before his fist connected, causing him to stumble.

He glared up at the monk, expecting to see mirth, which he would have sliced off his face in an instant. Instead, he saw fear.

'The cathedral is open to all,' the monk at the door said in a shaky whisper, blanching at the sight of steel. FitzUrse ignored him and brushed past, searching the gloom of the great cathedral for his quarry. His eyes lit on a huddle of men. 'North transept. By the high altar. Onward.'

He strode forward, heartened by the sound of purposeful boots on flagstones behind him.

'Becket! Traitor! You will come with us by the order of the King.'

'I am no traitor, Reginald. The traitors here are you and your friends. You are my sworn vassals yet you dare enter the sanctuary of Our Lord with swords drawn?'

'We are the sworn vassals of the King, above all other men!'

'And what about God? You insult Him by entering His house so armed?'

'Traitor!' FitzUrse accused again, unable to conjure a more ribald riposte.

'And what are you?' Becket taunted, pushing past two of his monks who were doing their best to shield him. 'A procurer! And I see the Lord Broc, the King's most senior whoremaster is here too. Good afternoon, Sir Ranulf. Has the King really sent his pimps to procure an archbishop rather than whores? He must think highly of you after all!'

FitzUrse roared with rage and rushed forward, his impetus enough to carry Morville, Tracy and Brett in his wake.

'Reginald, are you mad?' Becket's voice at last portrayed fear, but it only drove the knights on and broke the paralysed terror of Becket's men as half of them fled. Now it was four against four, although the knights had an army at their backs; the clerics had naught but an altar.

FitzUrse and Brett grabbed the priest. 'Tracy, bend over,' FitzUrse ordered. At Tracy's bewildered look, he explained further. 'We shall get him on your back, then carry him outside.'

'No!' Becket lunged at the nearby pillar, clutching it to his bosom as if his life depended on it.

FitzUrse burst into bellows of laughter as Brett tried to pull the Archbishop's grip from the pillar and Tracy attempted to heave the man away. Morville stood, sword raised to keep those clerics who had stayed under guard, whilst Broc and his men stood back, seemingly viewing the proceedings as a mummers' show.

FitzUrse flicked out his sword and caught the Archbishop's fur cap which he flung towards the altar, then smacked the holy man's rump with the flat of his blade. Becket roared in outrage and Tracy gave up the tug of war, dumping the Archbishop in an ungainly heap on the floor.

'Sire!' one of the monks, Grim, cried out, and escaped Morville to rush to his master's side.

Becket jumped to his feet, his face red, and confronted FitzUrse. 'You *have* gone mad, Reginald. You have lost what few wits you were born with! This is no way to treat any man, especially in God's house, never mind *me*. You swore fealty to me! Yet you make a mockery, not only of yourselves, but of My, *Our* Lord, and His sanctuary! Leave this place and do not return!'

In reply, FitzUrse took hold of the Archbishop's cloak and pulled the man closer. Before he could speak, however, Becket spat in his face.

'Unhand me, *pander*. You are not worthy to touch this cloth.'

'By God, men, if you do not shut him up, I shall rip the very head from his body,' FitzUrse roared. He let go his hold of the holy cloth and stood back to give himself room to swing his sword. Becket bent forwards, clasping his hands before his face in prayer, beseeching God to be ready to welcome him through the gates of Heaven.

Tracy lunged before FitzUrse finished his backswing. The monk – Grim – raised his arm to protect his master, but Tracy did not flinch. His blade glanced off the top of the Archbishop's head, sliced a deep gouge through Grim's upper arm, and parted the flesh of Becket's shoulder until he struck bone.

Grim screamed in agony, yet Becket barely paused in his prayers. 'Into Thy care, Lord, I commend my spirit.' He sank to his knees as the blood flowing from his wounds weakened him.

Tracy struck at his head once more, screaming as he swung his blade and the priest fell.

Tracy rested on his sword, the effort of such a heavy swing winding him, and Brett stepped forward.

Shrieking in rage, he thrust his blade at Becket, slicing the crown of his head clean away. Sparks flew, momentarily gracing Becket with a halo as the steel blade shattered. 'That's for William, my friend, the King's brother! He died of a broken heart when you refused his marriage. Now you have paid the price for his suffering,' Brett shouted.

Grim fell over his master, weeping, and Hugh Mauclerk – Morville's clerk – stepped forward. With the tip of his sword, he scraped the pinkish-white brain matter from the holy skull and smeared it over the bloody flags. 'That's one pesky priest who shall give no further trouble.'

Morville grabbed him, horrified at the callousness of his man – a man who had played no part in the actual deed. 'Hurry, we must depart.'

The knights turned to leave but paused at the glare of Broc and the horrified faces of the men who stood with him. 'What have you done?' Broc said.

'We have cured the King of his priestly troubles,' FitzUrse said, 'and you stood by and watched.'

Broc gritted his teeth in thought then said, 'Go. Back to Saltwood Castle. Take your belongings and ride north. Scotland may be safe for you.'

'And you?' Morville enquired.

'Me? I shall go to the King and plead your case.'

A man burst into the cathedral and hurried to his master. He hesitated at the sight before the high altar, then whispered into Broc's ear.

'Mandeville and Humez have beached. Hurry, you must leave.'

Chapter 4

12th June 2015

Friday night rehearsal over, the cast and crew of Knaresborough's amateur drama group – The Castle Players – headed out of the Castle Theatre to the Borough Bailiff for a pint or few and the debriefing. The rehearsal had not gone well and everyone had more anticipation for the alcohol than the discussion.

Helen Forrester's phone rang. She checked the display, then called to the others to order her a large gin and tonic and she'd catch them up.

'Hello?' she said into the phone, a mass of nerves as she prepared to hear the verdict on her proposal.

Half an hour later she joined the rest of the group in the pub. 'That was Richard Armitage from feva. They want us to perform *Knight of Betrayal*.'

'Bloody hell, that's fantastic news,' Paul Fuller said, 'well done, Helen!'

Feva was Knaresborough's annual festival of entertainment and visual arts, attracting authors, poets, musicians and artists of all persuasion from all over the country, as well as hosting a number of local attractions. It was quite a coup to have been chosen to put on a play as part of the event – and would be a definite boost to the Castle Players' status.

'They liked the idea of a play about Thomas Becket's death, given that the knights responsible hid out here afterwards.

Apparently the BBC set a play here about fifty years ago, but since then nothing. Most events have been centred on John of Gaunt or Isabella – Edward II's queen.'

'But Morville and the others are barely acknowledged here – did you know there's not one book about them in the bookshop?'

Helen shrugged. 'I guess the feva committee aren't so eager to brush history under the carpet.'

'Well, thank God for that,' Charlie Thorogood said. 'Otherwise we'd have been wasting our time with the play.'

'Charlie! We've only just started rehearsals,' Sarah Stoddard said.

'True, it's Helen who's put the time in writing the script,' agreed Sarah's husband, Dan.

'The main thing is we've got the green light,' Helen said. As writer and director, the hardest part of her role was to keep the egos of her actors in check, and she was well used to intervening before squabbles erupted into full-blown fights.

'We have until August to rehearse – that's two months and, judging by tonight's performance, we'll need every day of that.'

'Plus the sets to paint, props to source and costumes to make,' Ed Thomas said.

'And the sound and lighting programme, and equipment – don't forget that,' Alec Greene added.

Helen held her hands up. 'Yes, we have a lot to do, but it's nothing we can't handle. We've been given a grant of £500 to help with expenses so we can buy some props in.'

'What? They said yes? That's fantastic!'

Helen grinned. 'I know. We'll all pitch in with the sets and costumes. This is our big chance to play to a full house. If it goes well, we may get into Harrogate Theatre for a run too – maybe even York or Leeds.'

'Let's just focus on Knaresborough first,' Alec cautioned. 'Bad luck to count our chickens.'

'True enough, Alec. First things first,' Helen said. 'Speaking of the first things, what on earth went wrong tonight?'

Silence.

'Well?' Helen prompted. 'I can't be the only one who noticed. You know the lines, but it just didn't flow.'

Everyone looked at Charlie – who was cast as Thomas Becket – and Paul – cast as Henry II.

Finally Charlie spoke. 'It's difficult to get into the characters. They lived nearly eight hundred and fifty years ago, spoke a variation of French, and not only is there little source , but what does exist is contradictory. I'm struggling to get a sense of who Becket was as a man as opposed to an archbishop.'

'I second that – there is more information out there about Henry, but it focuses on his temper, dress sense, and marriage. Everything is just . . . one dimensional.'

'And there's even less known about the knights,' Ed, cast as Morville, said. 'They only feature in the history books on the night they assassinated Becket.'

Helen nodded. 'I had the same problems when writing the script, but I had hoped the dialogue would be enough to convey their characters.'

'We're not criticising your writing, Helen,' Charlie was quick to say. 'It's just that the twelfth century was so long ago and life and culture so different, we're struggling to get a handle on it.' He looked around the table for support, aware he'd inadvertently spoken for everyone.

'I'm finding the same,' Paul said. 'Royalty then was different to royalty now.'

'Well at least that's an easy one,' Helen said. 'Henry II was your quintessential dictator and warlord. Think Mugabe, al-Assad, Gaddafi, Hitler, Stalin et cetera.'

'But that's a simplification,' Paul persisted. 'Yes he was a dictator, but he didn't have total control of power over his subjects – he shared it with the Church and was second to God and, by association, the Pope. There is no situation or role today that compares.'

Helen nodded and finished her gin. Mike got up, took a couple of notes from the pile they had pooled together in the centre of the table and went to the bar to get the next round in.

'I have an idea,' Helen said. 'Sarah, are you free tomorrow?'

'Yes, I think so. Why?'

'Meet me at nine, we have some shopping to do before tomorrow's rehearsal.'

'What for?' Dan asked.

'You'll see.'

Chapter 5

'So what's this mysterious shopping trip about?' Sarah asked as Helen approached.

'Ah, wait and see,' Helen said, looping her arm through her friend's and leading her through the market square. 'To be honest I'm not sure if it's genius or madness but we're about to find out.'

'Now you really have me intrigued,' said Sarah with a nervous laugh. 'What are you up to?'

'Well, you know the new shop that's opened up on Kirkgate?'

'Which one? Oh, you don't mean the witchy one, what's it called, Spellbound?'

Helen laughed. 'Oh yes. Desperate times and all that.'

'Not that desperate, surely?'

'Did you not see them last night? They were so wooden they may well have been planted in Knaresborough Forest. We need to do something drastic to loosen them up and help them embrace Becket and Henry.'

'But spells, seriously?'

'No, not spells,' Helen said. 'We're here, come on.'

The smell hit them first, a mix of herbs and incense, and both women relaxed. A large display of crystals adorned the table in the middle of the shop which drew them closer, both of them compelled to touch the beautiful diodes, points and tumble stones.

They wandered around the rest of the filled interior; books, tarot cards, bags of herbs with appropriate spells, wands, dreamcatchers, all inspiration to their imaginations.

'Okay, I give up,' Sarah said, hands full of crystals, angel cards and incense that she felt she just had to have. 'What are we here for?'

Helen said nothing, but pointed up to the objects displayed on top of the bookcases.

'No, oh no, Helen, you can't be serious.'

'I'm very serious,' Helen said. 'No one is connecting with their characters, we've tried the conventional exercises – picturisation, sense memory, circle of concentration – but nothing is working. We have eight weeks to put on a play to wow feva, Knaresborough, and every visitor who pays good money to see us. How better than to ask the men themselves?'

'But a *spirit* board? They scare me, Helen.'

'We'll be fine as long as we're careful and responsible.'

'Good morning, ladies, I'm Donna.' A petite blonde woman dressed in purple, and with a genuine smile on her face approached them. 'I couldn't help but overhear, and you're right to be wary of the Ouija. The boards need to be used properly and with care, but if they are, they can be a powerful tool.'

'But isn't it like opening the doors to your home and inviting any passing stranger inside? Dead strangers I mean,' Sarah said.

'It is if you don't take precautions, but I don't let anybody buy one of these from me without full instructions to ensure that does not happen.'

'Which is the best one?' Helen said, studying the half dozen designs, all featuring the letters of the alphabet, digits 0 to 9, yes, no and – very prominently – the word goodbye.

'Whichever you feel drawn towards,' Donna said.

'That one,' Helen said, pointing at one with the Spellbound branding. 'I want yours.'

'Thank you.' Donna pulled a footstool out from behind the counter and plucked a board and planchette from the shelf. She went back behind the counter and rummaged through some paperwork to find a three-page sheaf of A4. 'Please read this carefully before you use it.' She put the paper, board and planchette into a black paper bag. 'It tells you everything you need to know to make sure you use the board safely.'

'That's a lot of advice,' Sarah said, still nervous.

'Not really, it basically says the same three things in a number of different ways. Be positive, protect yourselves, and close the board at the end of your séance.'

'Close the board?' Helen asked.

'Yes. Say goodbye. Make it clear that the session has ended and the spirit is no longer welcome.'

Helen nodded but said nothing.

'That's £30 please.'

Helen handed over her credit card, then Sarah emptied her hands of her own prospective purchases and paid for them.

'Are you sure this is a good idea, Helen?' Sarah asked as they walked to the High Street and the Castle Theatre.

'Nothing else has worked,' Helen said. 'It's different, we can have fun with it, and hopefully it can connect the cast with their characters.'

'By bringing forth their spirits?' Sarah asked.

Helen laughed. 'You don't believe that crap do you? There's no way Thomas Becket, Henry II and those knights will visit us. I just want the guys to open their minds and embrace their characters. It's all psychological. If they believe their spirits are with them, they'll become them – I just need them to break through whatever is blocking them at the moment. We don't have long and they need to be perfect or the Castle Players may as well disband. I'll do everything I can to make sure we pull this off.'

Chapter 6

'Henry has decided on Becket for Archbishop of Canterbury,' Helen said, her voice projecting throughout the empty theatre.

Paul and Charlie stood on stage, scripts in hand. 'So are they still friendly at this point?'

'At the beginning, yes, but Becket doesn't want the archbishopric – he realises that it will cause problems and it will be impossible to marry his loyalty to Henry with duty and service to the Church.'

'But if they're such good friends, why doesn't Henry listen to Becket?' Paul asked.

'Henry is a twelfth-century king – he listens to no man but himself,' Helen said. 'Basically, he's a dictator who believes he has a divine right to rule and is always right.'

'So, a typical man then,' Sarah said with a laugh, but accepted with good grace the playful thump on the arm from her husband, Dan.

'As I was saying,' Helen's voice projected once more, bringing the Castle Players to order. 'Henry makes Becket archbishop, despite him not being ordained as a priest. Becket has no choice but to make the best of it, and chooses his role as the Church's highest representative in England over friendship and Chancellor to King Henry II. He resigned as Chancellor . . .'

'But is this important?' Charlie asked. 'What does it have to do with his murder? I thought that's what the play's about.'

Helen sighed. 'It is, but it's also about the motivation and why a man who had been such a good and trusted friend of Henry's ended up assassinated in his name. This is where it starts. Making him archbishop was Henry's first mistake as far as Thomas Becket was concerned.'

'Oh,' Charlie said, nodding. 'I see.'

'From the top,' Helen said.

HENRY II (PAUL FULLER)
Thomas, 'tis my will and pleasure that thee succeed Theobald in the archbishopric of Canterbury.

THOMAS BECKET (CHARLIE THOROGOOD)
'Tis an honour too great, Sire. Why, look at me (indicates fine clothing). *I am hardly a man suited to the purity, poverty and abstinence of this holy office.*

'Okay, stop there,' Helen said. 'Paul, Charlie, this is a monumental request, you sound as if Henry is asking directions to Canterbury not appointing a new archbishop. Give me more – emotion, import, passion. Try again.'

HENRY II (PAUL FULLER)
No better man can I depend upon to act as mediator 'twixt King and Church. Together we shall bring England to glory.

THOMAS BECKET (CHARLIE THOROGOOD)
Sire, I would not gainsay thee, but consider it further, please. I would not the Church came betwixt us.

'Enough,' Helen shouted. 'Paul, Charlie, I'm still seeing and hearing you up there – I need to see Henry and Becket.'

'Well you're not going to see them two, are you? Not when we're dressed in jeans. It's not exactly medieval costume.'

'Costumes aside, you sound like Paul and Charlie, not Henry and Becket. We don't have long to get this right, and it could be our big chance.'

'Well, what do you suggest?' Charlie said, sounding irritated.

'Something a bit different,' Helen said. 'For all of us. We need to embrace the twelfth century – the culture, politics and the characters – and we need to do it quickly. Everyone on the stage, please, now. Paul, Charlie, will you bring that table into the centre? And we need chairs too.'

The octet of Castle Players sat around the circular table, most looking resigned to yet another game to release their inhibitions and take on the mantles of their characters. All but Helen and Sarah – they both seemed nervous, and Dan narrowed his eyes at his wife.

'What the hell is this?' Charlie exclaimed when Helen produced the black and purple spirit board and placed it in the centre of the table.

'You have got to be joking,' Dan said.

Helen looked at each of them in turn. 'No, I am not joking. We need to do something to channel these characters. We've tried most of the usual exercises and nothing's worked.'

'Well it's hard to play a man who's nearly eight hundred and fifty years dead,' Paul said.

'I agree, so why not ask for help from the men themselves?' Helen said.

'Assuming I believe in ghosts, which I don't,' Charlie said, 'why would their spirits come and talk to us?'

'As you pointed out yesterday, there are so few surviving accounts of their lives – and all contradictory – why wouldn't they want the truth of their lives told?' Helen said.

'I'm not sure about this,' Mike said. 'I don't like messing in things I don't understand.'

'It's okay, Mike,' Sarah said. 'The woman in the shop gave us loads of advice about how to use it properly and be safe.'

'Us?' Dan said. 'So this is what your secret shopping trip was about?'

'Helen asked me not to say anything,' Sarah said, refusing to look at him, 'not until she brought it up.'

'Since when do you put your friends before your husband?' Dan said, colour rising in his face.

'When that friend is her and her husband's director,' Mike said, staring at Dan.

'It's my fault, Dan,' Helen said. 'If you're angry at anybody, be angry at me, I'm the one who put Sarah in a difficult position.'

Dan looked at her, opened his mouth, then shut it again. He played Reginald FitzUrse and was still hopeful of a promotion to Henry II or Becket should Paul or Charlie prove unequal to their roles. He did not want to antagonise the script writer and director; he would continue the discussion with Sarah, later, in the privacy of their home.

Chapter 7

'Are we seriously going to do this?' Paul asked.

'Yes,' Helen said, 'and please try to be positive, or at least have an open mind.'

'Come on, Paul,' Sarah said. 'It might be fun and help us connect with the guys we're playing.'

'But we just— It's not something to be messed with,' Mike said.

'Have you used it before?' Sarah asked.

Mike hesitated.

'You have, haven't you?'

'Yes,' he admitted. 'At a party, years ago, these girls made one out of paper.'

'What happened?'

'Not a lot really, the glass they used instead of that thing,' he pointed at the triangular planchette, 'flew across the room and smashed.'

'Then what happened?' Helen asked.

'Nothing, we were all freaked out, so we burned it.'

'Somebody just flicked the glass,' Dan said with a smirk, 'to freak you all out.'

'Maybe.' Mike shrugged. 'But I don't see how.'

'You said it was at a party,' Sarah said. 'Were you all pissed?'

Mike grinned. 'Well . . .'

'There you are then,' Helen said. 'Stop worrying. I know what I'm doing. Are we all ready?'

'I suppose so,' Mike said. 'But we stop if things get too weird, okay?'

'Fair enough,' Helen said. 'What about the rest of you?'

The others shrugged or nodded with varying degrees of assuredness, which Helen took as assent. She placed her fingers on the planchette.

'Paul and Charlie, you have the two main roles, I'd like you to touch the planchette as well, then everyone else put your hands on top.' Helen said and waited until they'd complied.

'Okay, I'm going to protect us first – we don't want anything flung against walls,' she said with a smile at Mike. 'I call on our angel guardians and spirit guides to protect us here tonight.'

'Are you serious?' Dan asked, pulling his hand away.

'Yes, I am. Please, Dan, stay positive.'

'But angels and spirit guides?'

'Would you rather I called on the devil?'

'No, of course not!'

'Then let me carry on.'

'I'd rather we at least put the intention out there for angels, Dan,' Sarah said.

Her husband stared at her, then returned his hand to the tower of fingers on the planchette.

'Thank you, Dan,' Helen said. 'I call on our angel guardians and spirit guides to be with us tonight as we try to contact Henry II, Thomas Becket, and Sirs Morville, FitzUrse, Tracy and Brett. We ask that you surround us in a protective white light and facilitate contact with the spirits we are asking to communicate with.' She bowed her head and fell silent.

'Did they answer you?' Dan said. Helen ignored him.

'Henry Plantagenet, Thomas Becket, Hugh de Morville, Reginald FitzUrse, William de Tracy, Richard le Brett, I humbly beg you to join us this evening, your presence is welcome and we would be honoured if you felt able to help us tell your story.'

'Overdoing it a bit, isn't she?' Dan whispered to Sarah.

'Shush. She's speaking to medieval nobles, including a king. They would expect nothing less,' Sarah hissed back. Dan shrugged.

'Henry Plantagenet, Thomas Becket, Sir Hugh, Sir Reginald, Sir William, Sir Richard, will you speak to us? You are most welcome here.'

Everybody stared at the planchette. It didn't move.

'Now what, oh high priestess?' Dan said.

Helen glared at him.

'Maybe we're asking for too much at once,' Sarah said.

'That sounds plausible,' Paul said. 'Why not focus on Henry and Becket first?'

Helen nodded. 'Good idea. Okay, just Paul, Charlie and myself touch the planchette.'

'Why you, Helen?'

'I'm acting as medium, Dan. The notes from the lady in the shop said one person should be in control of the board.'

'And of course that's you,' Dan said under his breath.

'Pardon?'

'Nothing. By all means carry on.' Dan made an expansive gesture with his hands, leaned back in his chair and folded his arms.

Helen ignored him and looked at Paul and Charlie. 'Ready?'

They both nodded and Helen took a deep breath. 'I humbly invite Henry Plantagenet, King of England, and Thomas Becket, Archbishop of Canterbury, to join us,' she said. 'Are you there?'

The planchette moved to point at the word *yes* on the board. Everybody – including Helen – gasped in surprise and lifted their hands away.

'Who did that?' Dan said. 'Who moved it?'

Helen, Paul and Charlie looked at each other – all innocent.

'It must have been one of you,' Dan insisted.

'It wasn't,' Helen snapped. 'Shall we continue before whoever it is leaves in disgust?'

'I'd have thought both Henry and Becket would feel quite at home with this squabbling,' Ed said, breaking the tension.

Helen smiled, placed her fingers back on the planchette, and looked up at Paul and Charlie. 'Well boys?'

They glanced at each other, then followed Helen's lead and assumed the Ouija position.

'Who are you?'

The planchette moved almost immediately and pointed at the letter *H*, then to the *2*.

'Are you Henry Plantagenet, the king of England we know as Henry II?' Helen asked.

The planchette moved to indicate *yes*, then moved back to the empty space in the middle of the board.

'One of you is moving it,' Dan said. 'This isn't real, it can't be.'

'Shh,' said Paul.

'Thank you, Sire, for joining us, you are most welcome and we are honoured you have chosen to be with us this evening.'

No movement.

'You need to ask a question,' Sarah hissed.

Helen swallowed. Deep down, she hadn't thought this would work and hadn't prepared any questions.

Paul came to her rescue. 'Greetings, King Henry. I am Paul Fuller and have the very great honour of representing you in our play.'

Dan guffawed with laughter, and Sarah elbowed him to quiet him. Paul ignored him, and Sarah was the only one to see Dan's look of anger.

'I humbly beseech thee—'

'He's getting into the lingo now, at least,' Dan mocked.

'—to help me give a true and flattering portrayal of Your Majesty,' Paul continued. 'Would you be willing to help me tell your story?'

The planchette stayed still, then shot back to *yes*.

'My humble thanks, Sire.'

'If anyone says humble one more time, I'll sucker-punch them,' Dan said, then screamed as his chair shot backwards, tipping him over and dumping him on the boards.

'Nice try, Dan, grow up,' Mike said.

'That wasn't me.'

'So what, you *do* believe in ghosts now?'

'It wasn't me, the chair moved by itself!'

'In that case, I suggest you show more respect, Dan,' Mike said. 'You are disrespecting the first Plantagenet king of England, the head of one of our greatest dynasties.'

Dan said nothing, just glared at his fellow actors, then picked up his chair and gingerly sat down.

'Come on, Paul,' Sarah said, earning a more intense glare from her husband, which she ignored.

Helen glanced between the two of them, concerned at the marital discord on display, but pushed her worries to one side for now, and turned her attention back to the spirit board, Paul and Charlie. 'We all thank you for joining us, Sire,' she said, 'and apologise for our colleague's cynicism. He means no disrespect.'

Nothing. Helen looked at Paul, whose colour had drained to white.

'Forgive me, Your Majesty,' Charlie said into the silence. 'May I respectfully ask if your great friend, Thomas Becket is with you?'

The planchette vibrated, but did not move.

'Ask Becket,' Mike hissed and Charlie nodded.

'Thomas Becket, are you here with us?'

Again the planchette vibrated, then inched its way to *yes*.

'Welcome, sir,' Charlie said, swallowing. 'I am humbled that you have chosen to join us and ask you the same question, would you be willing to help me tell the true story of your later life?'

The planchette moved again to *yes*, then back to the empty place, then *yes*, back, *yes* over and over, gaining speed and ferocity.

Charlie, Paul and Helen snatched their fingers away all at the same moment. 'Hot,' Helen said, protecting her fingers under her armpits. 'It's just got hot.'

'But the room's freezing cold,' Sarah said.

Helen looked around and shivered. Sarah was right. 'When did that happen?'

'The first time the planchette moved,' Sarah said.

Nobody spoke. All wondered what the hell they'd been thinking.

'Our turn,' Mike said and everyone looked at him in surprise. He shrugged. 'Well, in for a penny, in for a pound, right? We've set this in motion, might as well follow it through. This is gonna be one kickass play,' he said, shuddered and placed his right forefinger on the planchette.

'Come on Sarah, Ed. Dan, are you up for this?'

With all attention on him, Dan coloured then added his finger to the planchette. 'If this goes tits-up, it's your fault, not mine.'

'Way to be positive, Dan,' Mike said. Everyone laughed and the atmosphere lightened.

'Come on, Helen, you're the medium, remember,' Sarah said. 'Give us your finger.'

More laughter, and Helen complied. She took a deep breath, glanced at Sarah, Dan, Mike and Ed, who all looked apprehensive with their fingers on the planchette, despite the laughter and bravado.

'Come on then, Helen, the surprise is killing me.'

'Not the best choice of words, Ed,' Alec pointed out.

Helen broke the ensuing silence. 'We are most grateful for the presence of King Henry and Archbishop Becket, and now respectfully ask that the barons and knights Morville, FitzUrse, Tracy and Brett also join us.'

The planchette quivered.

'Sir Hugh de Morville, are you here?'

Yes

'Sir Reginald FitzUrse . . .'

The planchette moved away then back to *yes* before Helen could complete her sentence and Dan smirked at her.

'Sir William de Tracy, are you here?'

Yes

'Richard le Brett, are you here?'

No

'No?' Sarah exclaimed. 'Why is my character the only one who says no?'

'If he's not here, how did he say no?' Mike asked. 'Ask again, Sarah.'

'Sir Richard le Brett, are you here?'

Yes

'Ask again, best out of three,' Alec suggested.

'Sir Richard le Brett are you with us?'

Yes

'Our thanks and gratitude to you all,' Helen said. 'History is vague and we know not the true circumstances leading up to and after that fateful day of 29th December 1170 . . .'

'Less speeches, more questions,' Dan interrupted.

Helen made to retort, then thought better of it. He was right. She looked at Charlie and Paul, then back at the planchette. They both understood and added their fingers to the others.

Helen took a deep breath, then said, 'Did you, King Henry, mean to order the assassination of Archbishop Thomas Becket?'

Board, planchette and table were thrown against the back wall of the stage, only missing the heads of the assembled company because all eight of them were thrust backwards from the epicentre of their séance, their chairs splintering as they fell against the wooden boards of the stage.

'I told you this was a bloody stupid thing to do,' Dan shouted, the first to get to his feet. 'We've messed with things that shouldn't be messed with. God knows what we've unleashed. Bloody stupid woman!' He looked around, then added, calmer, 'Where's Helen?'

The rest of the cast got to their feet, shocked, but only bruised, and looked around.

'There! She's down there,' Sarah called, pointing to the front row of seats.

'Shit,' Paul said, and jumped off the stage. 'Someone call an ambulance!'

Chapter 8

January 1170

'There she is, Cnaresburg Castle,' Hugh de Morville declared with evident pride as the knights emerged from the forest.

'God's blood, Hugh,' FitzUrse said. 'Even if Broc does turn the King against us, no bugger's going to get to us up there.'

The castle's keep, newly built from stone, perched atop the cliff, the deep gorge more of an obstacle than any man, or siege engine, would be able to conquer. The sight of it stunned the men; despite being of Norman descent and used to sights of the strongest castles in Europe, none were familiar with the rugged landscape of Yorkshire.

A deep, clear river sparkled in the late afternoon sunlight before them, above which the red-orange sandstone cliff towered. Trees and lush vegetation grew to the very banks of the River Nydde.

As the horsemen approached the river, a group of young goatherds looked up from their charges and spotted them.

'Á Morville,' they cried and a couple ran up the steep bank towards the town.

'Á Morville?' Tracy asked with a smile. 'You have them well trained.'

Morville shrugged, pleased at the welcoming war cry, but trying not to show it to his companions.

He led the way, his palfrey splashing through the shallow waters of the ford. 'Take care not to stray too far to either side, the waters can be treacherous,' he called to the following men. The knights glanced at each other and smirked, knowing full well that Morville was enjoying his role as overlord and the chance to assert the authority this status gave him, over Reginald FitzUrse in particular. All the men, not just the knights, but the accompanying men-at-arms of each house, had had more than enough of The Bear's overbearing bluster on their exhausting ride north.

'What are the defences on the far side?' FitzUrse called to Morville. 'I doubt you are as well-protected from the town as you are from the river.'

'The curtain wall is twenty feet high and four feet thick. The ditch is being deepened, but will be completed shortly, especially now that I'm here to oversee the work.'

'Towers?'

'At all four compass points, including those of the gates, although the southern tower is still under construction, as you can see.'

'It sounds like there is much still under construction.' Tracy laughed.

Morville turned in his saddle. 'When I was entrusted with the castle, it was little more than motte and bailey. That was seven years ago. In that time, the curtain wall has been raised, towers constructed, and the keep is now of stone. If you disapprove, you are more than welcome to continue to Scotland as Broc suggested and try your welcome there.'

Tracy held up his hands in mock surrender. 'No offence meant, My Lord. It is a wondrous castle.'

The others laughed and Morville screwed up his face in disgust, faced forward once more and spurred his palfrey up the steep bank of Brig-Gate.

*

'My apologies, My Lord,' Tracy whispered once they'd reached flatter ground. 'I did not mean to insult. It just struck me that we may be under siege here before long should the King take up arms against us.'

Morville glanced at him and sighed. He knew that Tracy was suffering larger and longer pangs of conscience than any of the others. He was not a killer by nature, merely a follower of killers.

'The King needed Becket stopped before he did any more harm. He was a traitor. Had we not taken care of the problem he would have revolted against not only the Young King, but King Henry himself. You know this to be true, we have talked of little else since we left Canterbury.'

'Bad things happen, William,' FitzUrse bellowed from behind them. 'We served our king well, he shall reward us.'

'And Broc?' Morville asked.

'Yes, he shall reward Broc as well,' FitzUrse replied with a grin. 'Handsomely, no doubt.'

'Broc won't . . . betray us?' Richard le Brett asked. As the youngest, of lowest status, and the man who had dealt the fatal blow, he had become the quietest, most timid of the quartet.

'He would no doubt attempt it should it be to his benefit,' FitzUrse laughed, 'but he hosted us at Saltwood Castle. He accompanied us and he supplied men-at-arms. We had more than enough between us, but he wanted a share of the glory.'

'And the loot,' Morville muttered. The four of them had helped themselves to gold plate and coin as they left. Broc and his men had taken everything else of value in the Archbishop's Palace, although had left the cathedral treasures. That would have been a sacrilege too far.

'He cannot betray us without betraying himself,' FitzUrse continued.

'But what of his suggestion for us to flee to Scotland?' Tracy asked.

FitzUrse bellowed laughter. 'His idea of a jest, is all.'

'A jest? To send us to a man who would gladly hang us as Englanders?'

'He has an evil sense of humour.'

'Á Morville! Á Morville!'

The knights' conversation was halted by the cheers as the townsfolk swarmed out of the alleyways to greet their returning overlord.

Morville raised his gauntleted hand in acknowledgement of the praise.

'They love you here,' FitzUrse said in wonder.

'No, they love the coin we will have to spend in the market. Look behind you.'

The knights twisted in their saddles to view the trailing men-at-arms. A force drawn from four houses.

'The population of Cnaresburg has just doubled.'

Chapter 9

Morville led the way over the drawbridge and through the north gate, and the knights clattered into the courtyard of the outer ward. Grooms rushed from the stables at the noise and the men jumped down from their mounts.

'Welcome to Cnaresburg Castle, My Lords,' Morville said. 'Make yourselves at home, we may be residing here for some time.'

The knights grimaced, all of them wondering the same thing: how had King Henry received the news of their deeds?

Morville led them through the inner gate to the bailey of the inner ward and pointed out the chapel and administration buildings. Nobody paid much attention. Once past the grandeur of the situation of the castle, the innards were nothing remarkable. The curtain walls and keep were the only stone edifices; all else was timber. Whilst it was apparent much building work had been undertaken, it was just as apparent there was a great deal still to be done.

'Helwise, welcome our guests,' Morville said to his wife, who stood at the door to the stone tower of the keep.

'Husband,' she acknowledged and nodded.

Brett, the last to be admitted, wondered at the faint trace of a smile on Lady de Morville's face at such an abrupt greeting.

Hugh de Morville flung open the doors to his great hall and stopped in shock. The force of FitzUrse blundering into his back pushed him onward and he took a couple of paces forward before once again coming to an abrupt halt. Cursing, FitzUrse, Tracy and Brett stepped around him before halting themselves and Brett understood the reason for the young Helwise de Morville's pleasure in spite of her husband's rude homecoming.

Morville remembered his manners and bowed to the men seated at the lord's table, instigating equivalent gestures from his companions. 'My Lords, I-I-I welcome you to my castle.'

'Not your castle, Morville, my brother's, King Henry. You are merely custodian here. For the present, at least,' said Sir Hamelin Plantagenet, Earl of Surrey. Seated at the overlord's place – Sir Hugh de Morville's seat – at the lord's table at the head of the hall, it was very clear to all present who held authority at Cnaresburg Castle this day. It was not Sir Hugh de Morville, Lord of the Manor of Cnaresburg, Baron of Burgh-on-the-Sands, Lord of Westmoreland.

Morville gathered his composure and greeted the other great men seated at his table.

Sir William de Courcy Lord of Harewood, and Morville's close neighbour Sir William de Percy Baron of Topcliffe, Lord of Spofford and Wetherby, sat at either side of Hamelin Plantagenet. None of the three appeared pleased to see the four travel-worn knights.

Morville looked around the bustling hall, nearly full he now realised, his awareness of his surroundings having been paralysed by his shock of seeing three great lords; three of King Henry's innermost and most loyal circle. He noted who else was present: Nigel de Plumton; Sir John Goldesburgh; Gamellor, Lord of the Manor of Beckwith; Morville's brother-in-law, William de Stoteville; and even his forester, Thomas de Screven. Everyone of any import in the vicinity was here, dining at Morville's pleasure, and cost, without his knowledge.

'H-H-How . . . ?' he stammered and FitzUrse poked him in the back. Morville drew himself to his full height and tried again.

'Forgive me, My Lords, it is of great surprise to find you here. We rode like the wind . . .'

'Yes,' Plantagenet drawled. 'From Canterbury. We heard. Then we sailed with the wind to ask you what the hell you were thinking.'

'Becket,' Morville began.

'Yes, Becket. Pray, enlighten us.'

'He was a traitor.' FitzUrse stepped forward, unwilling to allow Morville to plead his case on his behalf. 'He was planning to depose the Young King and, more than likely, King Henry himself. He was a man of great ambition, it is of no surprise to anyone that he had his sights on the crown of England. King Henry wanted him stopped. We stopped him.'

'You certainly did that,' Plantagenet said.

'How did King Henry take the news?' Morville found the courage to ask.

'Ahh, the pertinent enquiry.' Plantagenet pushed his trencher aside, crossed his arms and leaned forward on the table, glaring at the nervous knights.

He pulled back and addressed the men sitting either side of him. 'How would you say my brother took the news of the horrific murder of his closest friend of, what, twenty years?'

Courcy and Percy solemnly shook their heads.

'Panic-stricken,' Courcy said.

'I have never heard such lengthy lamentations,' Percy said.

Plantagenet nodded, then braced his elbows on the table once more and regarded the knights. The hall, filled with near two hundred men, was silent, every ear turned to hear the Earl's words.

'Panic. Lamentation. Yes. He then fell into a stupor, gentlemen.'

The knights winced. Whether at the news or the insult of 'gentlemen' was not clear.

'He fell into a stupor,' Plantagenet repeated. 'Took to his

bedchamber and naught was heard nor seen of him bar his groans of grief and constant prayers for the safekeeping of Becket's soul.'

As one, the knights paled and stepped back at this most dreadful news.

'He would admit no one, nor any succour; no flesh of any kind. And you know how my brother enjoys flesh.'

The lords at the table laughed, banging their fists on the wood. Henry had an appetite befitting a king; he loved his food and his women, and could never have his fill of either. This was serious.

The knights stayed silent.

FitzUrse glanced behind, but the door to the great hall was closed, with pikemen stationed to either side. There would be no escape that way. Just as there had been none for Thomas Becket.

'What say you to that, gentlemen?'

Morville fell to one knee, followed by Tracy, Brett and, after a pause, FitzUrse.

'My Lord, I am grievously wounded to hear such news. The King demanded vengeance on the Archbishop, our only aim was to obtain that for His Majesty.'

'He demanded action from Mandeville and Humez!' Plantagenet roared, leaping to his feet. 'He gave you no such instruction!'

'But My Lord . . .' Morville faltered as Plantagenet raised his eyebrows and scowled.

'The eve of the Great Council,' FitzUrse broke in. 'At supper, the King demanded vengeance from anyone who had the courage to obtain it. We had that courage. My Lord,' he added, casting his eyes down once more.

'Courage? Courage, is that what you call it? Stupidity to the utmost degree, say I! You broke the sanctity of Canterbury Cathedral! You killed an archbishop on his altar steps. An archbishop armed only with a hair shirt! How is *that* courage?'

A hair shirt? All four of the knights blanched. *He was pious after all?*

'My Lord, we attempted to take him peacefully,' Morville ventured, swallowing the lump in his throat at the unwelcome news. 'We did so without arms and without mail. He laughed at us and laughed at the King.'

'He *laughed* at the King?' Plantagenet asked.

'He did, My Lord,' FitzUrse said. 'So we regained our arms and returned for him. He refused to leave the cathedral, made it impossible for us to remove him, and taunted us. By taunting us, the King's men, he taunted the King. We could not permit that.'

'I see.' Plantagenet retook his seat. 'I see, well, that does shine a different light on things.'

'It does?' Tracy asked, speaking his first words since entering the hall.

'Well, it would had Ranulf de Broc not already made that clear.'

'My Lord?' Morville asked, confused.

Plantagenet laughed. 'It has been said that had my brother not been high-born, he would have made an excellent mummer, is that not so?'

Courcy and Percy looked at their trenchers and made no reply.

'Oh come now, My Lords, I hear the talk, we are amongst friends here. I ask you again, is that not so?'

Courcy relaxed and nodded. 'Yes, it has been said, My Lord.'

'Excellent. And what say you, do I have some of his skill?'

'Worthy of a prince,' Courcy said.

The knights glanced at each other in confusion, unable to understand what was happening.

'Oh stand, My Lords, stand.'

The knights regained their feet.

'My brother has to put on a show. He must appease the Pope, do you understand?'

The knights nodded, yet still appeared uncertain.

'*Before* he secluded himself, he sent messengers to Rome, and included details of his seclusion within his missives.'

The knights glanced at each other, now starting to understand. Or at least, they hoped they did.

'As long as Henry's messengers reach Pope Alexander first, this unfortunate incident shall be brought to an amenable close.'

'And if they are not first?' Morville asked.

'Well, then all Hell and the fury of Christendom shall descend on your souls.'

Chapter 10

Jack, the head steward of Cnaresburg Castle, placed dishes of thrice-cooked pork, onion and beans on to the lord's table and the hungry knights speared large pieces with their eating knives. For a while, all was silent as they sated their hunger and thirst.

FitzUrse was the first to sit back, signalling for more wine. 'That was quite a welcome,' he said. 'I thought it would end with our heads on pikes on the towers of the gatehouse.'

'I fear it was a near thing,' Morville said. 'Let us hope that the King's messengers are the first to give Pope Alexander the news.'

'They had me in fear and no mistake,' Tracy said, emptying his goblet which was immediately refilled.

'Am I to understand that you . . . killed the Archbishop, husband?' Helwise de Morville said.

'Hush, child.' Morville swept his hand to the side, catching Helwise on the side of her face and rocking her back in her chair. Her face reddened and her eyes filled, but she gave no other outward reaction.

'Hugh!' her brother, William de Stoteville, exclaimed in her stead from her other side and placed a comforting arm around his sister's shoulders.

Morville leaned forward and pointed his eating knife at him. 'Do not *you* disrespect me at my table, William, as does your sister.'

Stoteville gritted his teeth together to prevent his retort, knowing his sister would likely pay for it later.

Helwise shrugged his arm away and patted his knee with a small smile. Twenty years Morville's junior she had been his wife seven years, since she was nine, and although Morville had only taken his marital dues in the last couple of years, she already knew to recognise his moods and behave accordingly.

Despite the coldness in their marriage, she was glad of it; it had enabled her to not only remain in Cnaresburg, but run the castle and care for her town during her husband's absences, which were frequent and lengthy.

'Why do you think the lords did not remain to sup with us?' Brett asked, gallantly coming to his hostess's rescue. He gave her a small yet kind smile as soon as Morville's attention was turned.

'I fear they would withhold any outward show of favour until they hear of Pope Alexander's reaction,' Morville said and took a large gulp of wine.

'What shall we do should Alexander condemn us?' Tracy said, panic lacing his words.

'He shall not,' FitzUrse said with confidence. 'He would be condemning King Henry should he do so and would not risk making such a powerful enemy.'

'He may already view King Henry as an enemy,' Morville said. 'Remember I witnessed the Charter of Clarendon? It took away the freedom of the clergy and made them accountable in law to King not Church. Henry crowed about how he had beaten Alexander. I doubt the Pope took it lightly. He may see this as an opportunity for revenge.'

'God's wounds,' Tracy muttered, emptying another goblet; an action repeated by his fellow knights as they considered the possible implications of their deeds. 'No wonder the lords departed so hastily for Spofford.'

'Calm yourselves, Percy is past his prime, eighty years and more has he not, Helwise?' Morville turned to his wife who gave a curt nod. 'An old man enjoys the comforts of his own home.'

'And they'd supped their fill at your table, Hugh.' FitzUrse roared with laughter.

'Indeed,' Morville said, spearing another slice of pork.

'At least we need not explain ourselves further to them,' Brett said. 'And can rest and dine well after our ordeal.'

'Indeed,' Morville repeated and raised his goblet in a toast. 'Comfort, safety and sanctuary.'

The knights drank, as did Helwise and William, albeit reluctantly. They shared a quick glance acknowledging the hypocrisy of the toast to sanctuary.

A serving girl leaned between Morville and Helwise to place a pie of apple, damson and dates before them. Helwise ignored her husband as he – heading into his cups – fondled the girl's leg and rump at length.

'That will be all, Mable,' Helwise said, and the girl scurried away. Morville glared at his wife.

'Now I see why you insisted on coming to Cnaresburg, Hugh,' Tracy said, his words becoming slurred. 'Such a beautiful and young wife.'

Helwise glanced at him, grateful he had commanded her husband's attention.

'My wife is beautiful too,' Tracy confided very loudly. 'Although no longer young.' He laughed and drank again, then leaned forward to look past FitzUrse and Morville and addressed Helwise.

'She is with child,' he said, his face a picture of pride. 'Borne me two fine sons already.' He paused. 'Olion and Oliver, both knights themselves now. Fine men, the pair of them.'

'They are indeed,' Brett said. 'I last saw Oliver in Normandy before we departed for England. He has grown so strong, he bested me at a wrestle in no time at all.'

'Verily. A fine warrior,' Tracy said, holding his goblet up to toast but spilling most of its contents on to the sleeve of his tunic.

'Pomperi,' he said, oblivious, 'my beloved wife. I hope to see her again.'

His face fell, then he looked up. 'I *will* see her again, will I not, Reginald?'

'Without a doubt, William. Without a doubt.' FitzUrse pulled a passing serving girl on to his lap. 'Until you do, there are plenty here who would enjoy your attention, is that not so?' He nuzzled the young girl's neck.

'Of course, My Lord,' she squeaked before extricating herself and scampering back to the kitchens.

The table of knights roared with laughter. Even Tracy smiled, drained what was left in his goblet then stared at the table in morose silence.

Chapter 11

Helwise was awoken by fingers fumbling beneath her shift. Her heart sank as she realised her husband was already awake and had recovered from the excesses of the previous evening.

He had fallen asleep as soon as he'd lain down, but Helwise's relief had turned to irritation as the volume of his snores did not diminish throughout the night hours. She felt as if she had only just fallen into slumber and was not yet prepared for the new day.

She did not move or indicate she was awake, and kept her legs still and heavy, resisting her husband in the one way open to her. On occasion it had worked, but not this morn. Hugh de Morville would not be denied his wife.

With a groan of frustration, he flung aside the bed covers, rose and knelt over Helwise, pushed up her shift and forced her legs apart.

Helwise remained still and silent, taking no part in the act, then cursed herself as her body responded, despite her wishes and his sour breath.

She clasped her legs around her husband with a moan, who reacted in both strength and vigour until they cried out together.

Morville rolled away and levered himself off the bed. He poured a little water into a bowl, splashed his face, then pissed into the fireplace before donning hose, smock and cote.

'Hurry yourself, Helwise. I wish to hear the progress made on the tower and ditch and view the work done in my absence. You would be my guide.'

'Very well, husband,' Helwise said, reluctantly climbing out of bed. She wished for another hour or two of slumber, but knew this would hold no sway with Hugh.

She dressed in a long chainse with tight-fitting sleeves, then chose a dark-blue bliaut. It fitted snugly under her breasts, the voluminous skirts draping to the floor. She adjusted the sleeves until they were comfortable; closely tailored from shoulder to elbow then draping to the same length of the skirts.

After donning a coif to cover her hair, then adding the face-encircling barbette that Queen Eleanor had made so popular, she added a fillet around the top of her head to secure everything in place. She fastened her emerald-green cloak at her neck and hurried down the spiral stairs to join her husband at the south tower.

Helwise found Morville in the inner bailey, surrounded by smiths, ropewalkers, carpenters and wood-turners. He turned to study the complete towers of the east, north and west gates, then stared to the south. No gate here at the top of the cliff, but the new defensive watch tower was less than half the height of the completed structures.

'I had thought it to be raised higher by this time,' he said.

'The weather has been inclement,' Helwise said, 'making the quarrying difficult, affecting the mix of the mortar and turning the scaffolding treacherous. The masons have done well in the circumstances.'

Morville harrumphed and led the way through the doorway to climb the spiral staircase, then scrambled out on to the scaffolded platform at the top.

'My Lord,' the mason said in surprise, finished tamping down the stone he had placed, then laid down his tools. 'I bid you welcome.'

Morville nodded. 'How goes progress?'

'We are making the most of the break in the weather, My Lord.' He nodded towards the treadmill. 'That was damaged in the last storm, but as you can see is working once more.'

Morville said nothing, but watched the two men inside the contraption walking the wheels around. Presently, a plank carrying a load of sandstone rose over the edge of the platform and was manhandled on to the platform to be sorted by colour. The strongest dark-grey stone would be used for the facing and structure of the wall, which would be infilled with the reddish and softer yellow stones, giving great strength to the thick defences.

Morville ran his hand over the faced stone of a completed section and nodded in satisfaction at its smoothness.

He peered over the edge to examine the ditch below. More quarry than dry moat at this time, it was abustle with activity; men quarried stone, the rhythmic clanging of the masons' chisels facing the blocks for the inner and outer skins as well as the steps for the spiral stair was as effective as a drummer marking time for rowers or marching soldiers.

'It is quite a distance down, is it not, Hugh?' Helwise said at his side.

'It is indeed,' Morville said, happier now despite the lack of height of the tower. Any attacking force would be more than daunted by the height of the cliff and depth of the ditch, and even at this low elevation, he had a view of the valley for miles in all directions. Although there was plenty of ammunition for siege engines about the quarry, there was no flat ground for them to be situated and used against him. Cnaresburg Castle was in no danger from the south.

He glanced up at the sun, then turned to his wife. 'It is near time for dinner, Helwise, let us re-join our guests, see how they fare this day.'

'I am concerned for Sir William, Hugh. He seemed ill at ease last evening.'

Morville made a sound of disgust. 'He is weak of heart, blaming all but himself for his present circumstances.'

'He misses Pomperi,' Helwise said.

'Bah. He has two fine sons yet continues to bleat about his wife and the child she carries. It is unnecessary.'

'He is concerned, Hugh. It is good to witness.'

Morville glared at her, and she spoke no more but followed him away from the construction of the tower and back to the keep and great hall.

Chapter 12

19th June 2015

'Thank you, everyone, for coming,' Helen said. 'I know our last rehearsal was a little – strange – and am relieved none of you have given up on our production.'

'To be honest, Helen, we're all a bit freaked out,' Paul said. 'We can't explain what happened, and the possibility it was real scares the shit out of me, and I think everyone else, right guys?'

He got a few nods, but not from everyone, yet pushed on regardless. 'Was it worth dabbling in things we don't know, and to be honest, shouldn't know or have contact with in this life?'

'I appreciate your concern, Paul, and apologise to everyone – I had thought the spirit board was a way to allow you to tap into your psyches and your creative cores, to channel your characters, and become them when you're on stage. I honestly did not expect what happened.'

'How's your arm?' Alec asked.

'Broken wrist. It could have been a lot worse. Was anyone else hurt?'

'No,' Sarah said, 'just you.'

'Okay then, shall we start?'

Helen sat in the middle of the front row of seats; no gods, no boxes, no circles, just rows of seats on one level, more like an assembly hall than a theatre, yet it hosted a wide variety of acts and plays.

'We need to plan the sets – they'll take the most time to create – as you know it's mainly a two-hander between Henry and Becket, and they're rarely together geographically so we have to get creative.'

'Huh? How will that work?' Dan said.

'We need a set to represent a castle in Normandy for Henry's scenes, and Canterbury Cathedral for Becket's – and of course, most of their arguments and fallings out happened when they were separated by the English channel, and done by messenger, but that won't work in a play.'

'So what do you suggest?' Ed asked.

'One set split into two. The left-hand side as the audience looks on will be a Norman castle's great hall, the right-hand side Canterbury Cathedral. Most of the play will focus on these two locations – often at the same time.'

'But how will that work?' Sarah asked. 'We can't have two locations on stage at the same time.'

'I think we can – one stage, two locations. Henry in his, Becket in his, and use lighting to distinguish between the two. So when Henry makes Becket archbishop, the Norman castle and Henry are spotlighted, whilst Becket and Canterbury is dark. Then when Becket denounces his chancellorship, Canterbury is lit and Normandy dark. The lighting will switch between the two, following their dialogue. Is that possible, Alec?'

'Yes, absolutely. It will take quite a bit of setting up to programme, but there shouldn't be any problems.'

'Great,' Helen said. 'What about sets? Do we have enough time?'

'Just about,' Ed said. 'But they'll be rough – I can't go too detailed in the time we have. I think we can manage with one backdrop in a masonry design, so we can use it for the final scene too, then use different furniture and props to show the difference between castle and cathedral.'

'Okay.' Helen paused, knowing she had to ask the next question. 'So, does anybody feel any ill effects after what we did last week?'

'Aside from your broken wrist, you mean?' Alec said.

'Well, yes,' Helen said.

Silence.

'We didn't close the board,' Sarah said. 'The woman in the shop, Donna, said we had to close the board.'

'I think the board closed itself, babes,' Dan said, and Sarah glanced at him in annoyance at the annoying pet name.

Chapter 13

THOMAS BECKET (CHARLIE THOROGOOD)
Great Hall, Archbishop's Palace, Canterbury Cathedral.
So here I be, yesterday a layman, today the Church's highest authority in the land. What is my friend Henry thinking? And why does he not take my advice in this of all things?
(Sits at desk with quill, ink pot and parchment)
I may have no say in the archbishopric, but I shall resign as Chancellor, if only I could find the words to express my ire at Henry.

'Okay, stop there, Charlie,' Helen called. 'This is where we need to get to know Becket as a man. Who is he? What's his character?'

'Why don't you hold another séance and ask him?' Dan said, sarcastic as ever. Helen glared at him, then softened.

'Not one of my better ideas, I admit,' she said. 'Where is the board, anyway, has anyone found it? I think we should burn it.'

Dan look surprised. 'I thought you'd taken it.'

Helen shook her head. 'Not me, anyone else?'

Sarah, Mike, Ed, Alec, Paul and Charlie all shook their heads.

'Well, never mind, I'm sure it will turn up,' Helen said and brought her attention back to Charlie on stage.

'Becket's an important man. Up until now he's been the closest man to the King, Charlie.'

Charlie nodded. 'And now he's a priest, with no choice about the matter, I get it,' he said.

'Do you? He likes the finer things in life – clothing, food, hunting, women,' Helen said.

'Should fit right in then,' Paul said with a laugh. 'The bishops can go hunting together!'

'Ah, that they may have done, My Lord. But that shall not follow now I am the Primate of All England.'

'That's it, Charlie! You're getting it – you sound just like Becket,' Helen said, striking her knee with her good hand in place of clapping.

'My thanks, fair maiden,' Charlie said, bowing to his director.

'Thomas, my friend, thee must leave the ladies of the kingdom alone now,' Paul said, mounting the steps to the stage.

'Ah, so that is why thee foisted this most unwelcome honour on me. Thee is scared of the competition!'

Paul laughed and clapped his friend on the back. 'Not at all, Thomas. With thy help I shall bow the Church to my will and the will of England. No more of this petty squabbling that has become so arduous.'

'But Henry, thee has given me a great duty. As Archbishop of Canterbury, I must serve God above all else.'

'Thee serves me, Thomas,' Paul said. 'Me, thy King.'

'Of course, Sire,' Charlie said. 'I serve thee after God.'

'Thomas, I warn thee now, consider thy actions with care,' Paul said, balling his fists. 'I have not risen thee so high to stand against me. That does not follow. Does thee hear me, Bishop?' The last word was a sneer.

'Verily, Sire, and I shall bring all my powers to the task of tallying my spiritual duties with those demanded by thee.'

Paul opened his mouth to retort but was interrupted by clapping from the auditorium.

'This is going to work, isn't it?' Dan said. 'This is really going to work.'

Helen grinned. 'Oh yes, and a great bit of improv, guys. Can we try again with the scripts now? Scene three, from the top.'

Paul moved back to his position, and Charlie readied himself to restart his monologue.

THOMAS BECKET/CHARLIE THOROGOOD
I cannot fathom why my king has forced this upon me. Archbishop of Canterbury and Chancellor of England? Nay, 'tis too much, how do I reconcile such conflicting differences in my duties? I cannot.

'Hold it there, Charlie,' Helen said. 'You're wooden again.'

'Maybe it's the monologue,' Sarah said. 'It just isn't natural. Why don't you combine this scene with Paul's monologue in scene four? Have them both on stage and interacting – we can use that trick with the lights and sets you talked about.'

Helen pursed her lips in thought, then nodded. 'Okay, let's try it. Just improv for the moment and I'll rewrite.'

'Sire, 'tis with great reluctance, with not fear nor favour, that I must tender my resignation as your Chancellor,' Charlie said, pretending to write as he spoke. 'I find my pastoral duties too great to be able to fully apply myself to both positions.'

Paul crossed to the table and grabbed a piece of paper. 'Need a prop,' he said by way of explanation, then retook his position, cleared his throat and pretended to read.

'By God's eyes,' he exclaimed. 'I am betrayed and by my greatest friend in the nation! Is he now to be my most formidable enemy?' Paul appealed to the audience, arms spread wide.

'I fear I have angered my king,' Charlie said, head in his hands, then he sat up straight. 'But *he* has brought us to this pass.' He stood and approached the audience, putting Becket's case forward.

'Did I advise him to follow this road? Nay, I did not. Did I not warn him against taking this step? Indeed I did. Did he listen?' he said, voice rising, then softened once more. 'Of course, he did not.' Charlie gave a small laugh and shook his head.

Paul stepped forward. 'Betrayed!' he shouted. 'Betrayed by my most faithless friend! Whom now shall I trust? Who now is deserving of their king's favour?'

Silence.

'Indeed,' Paul said softly. 'No man in England is worthy of my faith, no man but myself.'

'I don't think they need that rewrite, Helen,' Dan said. 'They seem to be doing pretty well on their own.'

Helen nodded. 'Well done, guys, time for the pub, first round's on me.'

Chapter 14

The Borough Bailiff was one of the oldest pubs on the High Street. Named for the stewards who collected the rents for their lords, it was friendly, down-to-earth and a favourite of the Castle Players.

'Same again?' Dan asked and grabbed a twenty from the pooled money in the centre of their long table.

'Keep 'em coming, mate,' Mike said and laughed.

'Are you okay, Mike?' Sarah asked.

'Fine, Sarah, just peachy,' Mike said, leaning back on the bench seat and dropping his arm along the back of it. 'They did well today didn't they?' he added, leaning into Sarah's shoulder.

'They did. Though I don't think Helen is too pleased that her script went out of the window.'

'Too bad. The improv came across natr . . . nature . . . smoothly,' Mike said.

'Hmm.'

'What's wrong?'

'Well, you don't think it had anything to do with that spirit board, do you?' Sarah asked quietly.

'No, that was just a bit of silliness.'

'But the way we all fell! Helen broke her wrist – that's more than silliness.'

'Power of suggestion,' Mike said, finding it easier to get his words out with a little concentration. 'That's all, don't worry about it.' He stroked Sarah's hair and left his arm about her shoulder.

'Get your hands off my wife.' Dan slammed pints of bitter and lager on the table.

'Sorry mate, nothing meant,' Mike said, lifting both hands in supplication.

'Like hell there wasn't!'

'Hey, settle down guys,' Paul said. 'We're all friends here.'

'This bastard's getting far too friendly with my wife,' Dan said, leaning over the table towards Mike.

'Well, maybe you should treat her better,' Mike said.

Silence.

'What the hell do you mean by that?' Dan's voice was low and measured, and Sarah panicked.

'Nothing, Dan, he doesn't mean anything, he's just had too much to drink.'

'And why are *you* defending him?' Dan switched his ire towards his wife. 'Are you sleeping with him?'

'Dan!' Sarah said, shocked. 'Of course not.'

Dan stood upright. 'Yeah, now I see it, the pair of you have been too pally for far too long. And you enjoyed the kiss in the last play far too much. I see it now, you've been banging each other since then, haven't you?'

'Dan, how many times?' Sarah said, exasperated by not only having this fight again, but in company. 'It was a stage kiss, we're actors just as you are. There was nothing more to it.'

'Yeah, I bet,' Dan sneered.

'Dan, calm down, mate,' Mike said. 'You're embarrassing yourself.'

'Embarrassing? You're pawing my wife and call *me* embarrassing?' Dan lunged across the table and grabbed the front of Mike's T-shirt. The table collapsed, beer foaming over the carpet as Sarah screamed.

'That's enough!' the landlady shouted. 'Get him out of here!'

Alec and Ed had already jumped up to grab Dan. He shook

them off and slapped Sarah. 'Whore!' he shouted. Alec and Ed caught hold of his arms and wrestled him out of the pub.

Helen pulled Sarah into a hug.

'I'm so sorry, I'm so sorry,' Sarah said. 'I don't know what's got into him lately. This isn't him, it really isn't. Yes he can be a prick sometimes, but not like this.'

'I'm sorry, Sarah,' Mike said. 'I was just winding him up, I didn't mean . . .'

'I think you've said enough, Mike,' Helen said.

'No,' Sarah said. 'Mike's right, they take the piss out of each other all the time.' She reached out a hand and clasped Mike's forearm. 'It's not your fault, it's Dan. I don't know if something's happened at work or what, but he's been in a right mood for ages.'

'What's happening out there?' Helen said, trying to peer through the window in response to a crashing sound.

'I don't know, but I don't think I'm the best person to go and find out,' Mike said.

Helen nodded. 'I'll go. Mike, you and Charlie look after Sarah, okay?'

Both men nodded and Mike and Sarah sat down, Mike's arms around Sarah as she sobbed into his chest.

'I'll help clean this mess up,' Charlie said. 'And pay for the damage.'

'Charlie, no, I should do that, it's my fault,' Sarah said through gasping breaths.

'No it isn't,' Charlie said. 'Quite the opposite. Anyway, it'll come out of the Castle Players' fund, not my own pocket.' He winked at Sarah and went to attempt to placate the landlady.

Chapter 15

February 1171

'You are joining us?' Morville asked his wife as she entered the great hall, dressed in a forest-green bliaut over a sky-blue chainse.

'I am,' Helwise replied. 'I have been training a new merlin, she has done well on her own. I should like to try her in a full hunt.'

Morville nodded and the men shifted on the benches to make room for the lady of the castle to sit. The four knights had been joined by Helwise's brother, William de Stoteville; Gamellor, Lord of the Manor of Beckwith; Sir John Goldesburgh and Sir Nigel de Plumton.

No lord's table this morning; the knights had gathered around one of the low tables where they had more room to huddle together to plan the hunt. Warmed by a roaring fire, in front of which half a dozen greyhounds stretched, spirits were high and all were looking forward to the day's activity.

FitzUrse helped himself to another hunk of bread and lump of cheese as Thomas de Screven, the forester and head huntsman, strode into the hall, accompanied by two very happy looking lymers. The dogs rushed over to the fire to greet the greyhounds and Screven joined the knights and Helwise.

'Well?' Morville asked.

'A white hart, My Lord, in Haya Park. Twelve points. I have been keeping an eye on him for some time, he is a fine beast.'

'And you have his trail?' FitzUrse asked.

'Yes,' Screven replied and unrolled a scroll depicting the hunting grounds. 'He is in this area here,' he indicated the eastern quadrant, 'near Ferrensby.'

'Not far from Spofford,' Morville said.

'Yes. I met with Sir William's man, the Baron is on his way here to join you.'

'Excellent,' Morville said. 'I had feared he would not accompany us, I have received no reply to my message.'

'Another of his jests,' FitzUrse said with a scowl. 'He has been spending too much time in the company of Hamelin Plantagenet.'

'God's blood, they had me going,' Tracy said.

'Yes, you looked as if you had soiled yourself,' FitzUrse said.

'I think you all did,' Goldesburgh said, and the company of nobles roared with laughter. FitzUrse took a moment, then his colour calmed and he joined in the merriment.

'By God, he had us going,' Morville said, repeating Tracy's earlier words. 'I surely thought King Henry wanted our heads.'

'No, we served him well by cutting out the canker of England.'

'Henry's heroes,' Helwise said.

'Henry's heroes! Hear that, My Lords? We're Henry's heroes! All is well, we shall soon return to Normandy and to our king's side.'

'To our king's right hand,' FitzUrse corrected. 'We are the best of his knights now. To Henry's heroes,' he toasted, raising his goblet high.

The men and Helwise drank, with varying degrees of enthusiasm, then Morville brought their attention back to the business of the day.

'What better way to celebrate our great feat than to bring down a white hart? That rarest of beasts, his head can go right there.' He pointed at the far wall behind the lord's table. 'He will grace Cnaresburg Castle and boast of our success for generations to come.'

'I shall drink to that,' Tracy said, upending his goblet once more.

'Which way is the beast headed?'

The men turned as one, then stood to greet the aged William de Percy, Baron of Topcliffe. Helwise curtsied.

'I bid you welcome, My Lord,' Morville said, and Percy crossed the room to place a gallant kiss on Lady Morville's hand.

'Lady Sybil sends her regards, Helwise, alas her hunting days are behind her, but she bids you be successful and teach these men a thing or two of the chase,' he said with a twinkle in his eye.

'I shall do my utmost, Sir William,' Helwise said and Percy patted her hand. Their families had known each other for many years, and Percy was as fiercely protective of her as he was of his own daughters.

Trying not to show his irritation, Morville called for more bread and cheese as well as more flagons of Rhenish for his esteemed guest, then ushered Percy to the central position on the bench facing the fire.

The others shifted once more to realign the pecking order, and Percy sat down, raising his eyebrows at Screven.

'I spotted him here, My Lord, heading north,' the huntsman said, pointing at the chart. 'I suggest relays of hounds at these points.'

'Hmm,' Percy said. 'Put one of the relays there.' He indicated the place he meant. 'That terrain is rough, he may bear west for flatter, faster ground.'

'As you wish, My Lord.'

Screven bowed to Percy, then again to Morville, before calling the dogs to heel and exiting.

'Your marshal has your mounts ready?' Percy asked Morville.

'Yes, My Lord.'

'Then let us depart. Tally-ho!' He raised his goblet and the men and Helwise toasted to the success of their hunt.

*

Horns announced the nobles' departure from Cnaresburg Castle, warning the townsfolk that a horde of horsemen would soon be tramping through the marketplace and up the High Street towards Haya Park.

Traders and tradesmen scurried to shift carts and stalls to expose a thoroughfare through the centre of the marketplace, which was soon turned to chaos. The nobles were a clash of colour in their finery, each trying to outdo the other in their garishness: Morville in blue and white, Tracy red and white, and Brett and FitzUrse in red and yellow. Percy even had his courser, smaller than the destriers ridden in war, but a powerful beast nonetheless, decked out in blue and yellow to match his cloak.

The local butcher had a battle to keep the hounds from his wares; although well-trained, the dogs were hungry and excited at the prospect of the hunt, and the smell of fresh, even less-than-fresh meat, proved to be too much. Screven's shouts and blows of his horn to keep his charges in order merely added to the confusion, and the townsfolk, bar the butcher, revelled in the spectacle; cheering and applauding their lords as they passed. They knew that a hunt meant a feast later that day, with a surplus of leftovers to be distributed amongst the commoners of Cnaresburg.

Hugh de Morville, as overlord of Cnaresburg, basked in the glory and love shown, waving and showering the spectators with quarter-pennies. Thanks to his wife and her family, the de Stotevilles, who had lived here since the days of King William, he was well respected in this town and surrounds, and his wedding day had been one of the best of his life; principally because he had been awarded the custodianship of Cnaresburg Castle by a generous King Henry.

As the nobles walked their mounts away from the merriment, their minds turned to the fynding, wondering how long Morville's lymers, the best breed of dog for tracking, would take to find trace of the white hart.

Their mirth was cut short by the tolling of the church bell and the men glanced at each other in consternation as the peals added up. Ten. Twenty. Thirty. Announcing the death of a man. A local resident? Or had news of Thomas Becket reached Cnaresburg?

Chapter 16

'How is Pipsqueak now we are away from the hounds?' Helwise called over to Richard le Falconer.

He raised the wicker cage perched before him on his saddle so his mistress could see the small brown-grey merlin inside. 'She is well, My Lady. Has been since we hooded her and she could no longer see the lymers.'

'Poor thing, those dogs scared the feathers off her.'

'She's not used to seeing so many at once excited for the hunt, My Lady.'

'True. Well, let us hope she gets used to them soon.'

'Aye, My Lady. 'Tis a pity we could not go with the main hunting party, that white hart would be a sight to see and no mistake.'

'But a shame to see such a fine beast brought down for the table,' Helwise said. 'I am gladdened we had need of taking a different path, Pipsqueak needs open ground to hunt.'

Richard le Falconer made no comment and they rode in silence until they reached their usual larking grounds to the west of Haya Park.

Falconer reached into the cage, pulled the falcon out and unhooded her. The small bird of prey squeaked as soon as she laid eyes on Helwise – and continued squeaking. Even her small brain knew the appearance of the lady of the castle meant food, and she flew to Helwise's gloved fist to receive her first treat of a one-day-old-chick's foot.

Helwise raised her arm, the falcon's cue to start hunting. Pipsqueak launched, then swooped, flying low to the ground to flush out her first prey: a meadow pipit. Chasing and gaining height on the bird, Pipsqueak then dived at a seemingly impossible speed, and her talons plucked the unfortunate bird out of mid-air and brought it back to Helwise to be rewarded with another chick's foot.

Having been hand-reared and trained from the egg, Pipsqueak viewed Falconer as her father and Helwise her mother. She had not worked out that she would get more to eat for less effort if she simply feasted on the birds she caught.

'She's doing well, My Lady – a dozen larks and a couple of pipits in the last hour alone.'

Helwise smiled with pride, then gasped and stared at the treeline. A white hart bounded out from the trees, gracefully making ground at high speed, and dashed across the open moorland before making a sudden direction change and racing for the nearest trees to the north.

'He's magnificent,' she said. 'So handsome.'

'My Lady!'

Helwise glanced at Falconer in irritation.

'They're on the chase, that means—'

'The hounds!' Helwise scoured the sky, searching for her bird and knowing that if she did not secure her and hood her before the merlin falcon saw the dogs, they may well lose her.

Too late. The lymers and greyhounds, hot on the scent of the hart, disrupted the peace as they chased hard, followed by the hunting party of nobles.

'My Lady!' Falconer called, and Helwise returned her gaze upwards, to see a confused and panicking Pipsqueak launch a new dive.

She held out her fist, tapping it, while Falconer threw her a chick's head to tempt the falcon, but Pipsqueak picked up none of the visual cues, focusing instead on the object of her dive. The feather in the cap of Sir Hugh de Morville.

Talons outstretched, Pipsqueak arrowed in on her prey, grabbed what she thought to be a songbird, then struggled to lift the heavy woollen headwear.

She grounded amidst flying hooves and the shouts of an infuriated baron, and hopped in a desperate attempt to release the woollen encumbrance and take off to safety.

'God's wounds!' Morville shrieked. 'That bloody rat of a bird took my cap!' He rubbed his head, refusing to acknowledge the pain and shock of the strike from a six-ounce bird diving faster than the speed of a shot crossbow bolt; at least before his fellow knights. Helwise would hear more of it later, in private.

'Pipsqueak!' Helwise screamed, and ran over to the mêlée to rescue her youngest and favourite falcon.

'Get back, woman, do you want to be trampled?' Morville accented his warning with a flick of his crop. Helwise flinched to save her face from its sting.

Morville moved away from Pipsqueak. 'Retrieve my cap, Helwise, and train your bird better.'

Helwise rushed to Pipsqueak and untangled her sharp talons from the cap. The falcon hopped on to her fist and she passed the hat back to her husband.

'She is but a young bird, Hugh. She has not flown with the hounds before, they scare her.'

'Bah! A hunting bird scared of hounds? You'd do well to wring its neck.'

'No!' Helwise stepped back, away from her husband, her free arm held out in defence of Pipsqueak. At Morville's glower, she added, 'Begging your pardon, My Lord. I shall continue with her training. She is a good hunter – near two dozen larks for the table already.'

'Hugh,' FitzUrse called, 'we are losing the hart!'

'Hmpf.' Morville glared at his wife a moment longer, then pulled his courser's head around, kicked, and re-joined the chase.

Once the hunting party was out of sight and hearing, Helwise launched Pipsqueak once more.

'She missed! That's the first one she hasn't taken,' Helwise said as the falcon recovered from her unproductive dive, hugged the ground for a few wingbeats, then soared once more.

'And again. What's wrong? Do you think she's hurt?' Helwise asked Falconer.

'No, she would not be hunting if she were hurt. She's just unsettled.'

'We'll call it a day, then. Give her a rest.'

'Best to let her catch one first, else she'll learn she does not need to hunt to be fed.'

'Just this once?' Helwise implored.

Richard le Falconer shook his head. 'Sorry, My Lady, these birds are lazy and will not hunt if there is no imperative to eat. Best to wait and give her time, else your husband *will* wring her neck.'

Helwise nodded, knowing he was right, and examined the sky for a glimpse of Pipsqueak. 'She's diving,' Helwise said, excitement and apprehension inflecting her words; if Pipsqueak did not catch a lark soon, her future looked short.

Both Helwise and Falconer held their breath as Pipsqueak stretched her talons and snatched the skylark out of the air.

'Yes!' Helwise shouted, jumped and clapped her hands in exuberance, then turned and hugged Richard le Falconer.

'My Lady,' he reproached, stepping back.

'Oh, I beg your pardon, Richard. But she's done it, my little Pipsqueak has done it!'

She turned sideways on to the bird to make herself appear smaller and stretched out her right arm. Pipsqueak dropped the skylark into her waiting hand then circled round to fly on the wind and landed on Helwise's gloved left fist.

Helwise dropped the dead lark into her hunting bag and rewarded Pipsqueak with a full chick, squeezing the yolk from the head before offering the meal.

Richard le Falconer took the hunting bag from Helwise and stowed it on his horse, then returned with Pipsqueak's cage. The falcon hopped inside to finish tearing the chick apart and swallowing.

Chapter 17

Morville caught up his fellow nobles just as the chase ended. He saw the hart turn to face them – at bay and ready to defend himself against his pursuers.

He was a magnificent creature, standing taller than a man; his proud head with the dozen points lifted high, nostrils flaring, eyes staring and ears flicking at every bark of the restrained hounds.

The nobles spread out, surrounding the creature, and Morville glanced at Percy. Despite being the host, he indicated with a hand that the elderly Percy should take the kill.

William de Percy acknowledged the honour of the mort with a small nod, then drew his sword and walked his courser forward.

The hart took a couple of steps back, but stopped at a halloo from Tracy behind him.

Percy came on, drew his sword high, then slashed at the animal's throat, immediately backing up his courser to avoid the fountain of blood.

In silence, the hart fell to its fore-knees, his frightened eyes already dulling, then collapsed to the ground to the cheers of the gathered noblemen.

Morville was the first to congratulate Percy on the kill. 'It will make a fine course tonight, Hugh,' Percy said. 'I hope your cook can do it justice.'

Morville swallowed at the insult – etiquette dictated that the man who made the kill should host the resultant feast; they should be dining at Spofford Castle tonight not Cnaresburg – but he refused to let any sign of it show on his face or in his voice. 'Adam shall make a fine job of it, My Lord. Will you be gracing us with your company?'

Percy nodded. 'I shall.' He wheeled his courser around and cantered in the direction of Spofford Castle, leaving Morville to preside over the unmaking.

Screven stepped forward, unsheathing his knife, and began the job of dissecting the beast, starting with its guts before skinning it.

Once the hart had been unmade and the haunches of bloody meat and the proud head piled on to the small cart that had followed the nobles, Screven began the curée to reward the hounds.

He soaked stale bread in the blood of the hart, then mixed it with the intestines and pushed the resultant porridge into the gaping hole of the hide.

The dogs ran in excited circles, but their base instincts had long ago been beaten out of them and they held back until the sound of Screven's horn gave them permission to eat.

Morville watched the mêlée with interest – the deer carcass under the roiling mass of hungry dogs having a strange fascination – before he pulled the head of his courser around and led the way back to Cnaresburg Castle. He caught and rode past Helwise with no acknowledgement, and she fell in beside her brother, William de Stoteville.

Stoteville reached over and placed a hand on his sister's arm. He held no regard for Morville as a man, yet had a great deal of respect for his titles, in particular the barony of Burgh-on-the-Sands.

'Do not fret, Helwise. He will not be here long. There have been no repercussions to his deed and he will surely re-join King Henry in Normandy before too much time passes.'

Helwise smiled at him. 'It cannot come soon enough, Brother.'

He gave her arm another squeeze, then withdrew it. They both knew well the realities of marriage. Helwise would have to bear her husband's presence – whatever his demands – for as long as he chose to remain in Cnaresburg. Then she would be free to enjoy her position as Lady of the Castle until Morville deigned to return once more.

'William, what's happening?' Helwise asked, sitting straighter in her saddle and looking about her at the near empty High Street. 'Where is everyone? It's market day.'

William said nothing, but nodded his head towards the marketplace ahead. The townsfolk stood in silence, watching Morville and the others parade towards the imposing towers of the northern gate to Cnaresburg Castle.

One or two people smiled at the Stotevilles as they rode past, but there was none of the usual welcome. Whilst Morville was accepted as overlord, the Stotevilles were loved here, having lived amongst and advocated for these people for generations. Helwise was used to greetings, cheers and even the occasional posy of riverside flowers when she was about Cnaresburg. She looked to William in consternation.

'It appears that the news has reached Cnaresburg,' he said, his face grim as rotten fruit was thrown at the mounted noblemen ahead. Morville pulled his horse up and shouted at the assembled crowd.

'Murderer!' a young boy shouted. 'You murdered the Archbishop! May you rot in Hell!'

Morville jumped off his courser and forced his way into the crowd, reappearing with his fingers clasped around the ear of a young boy.

'Robert Flower!' Helwise gasped. 'Oh no.' Robert was a strange young boy – wiser than his years – whose outspoken ways often got him into trouble, yet Helwise – and most of the town it had to be said – had a soft spot for the young tearaway. Whatever trouble he got into or caused, there had always been good reason – at least in the boy's mind – whether it was stealing bread to give to a starving family or stealing cloth from Tentergate to present to his mother for a new gown. The people of Cnaresburg held him in a kind of exasperated regard.

Morville struck the lad, hard, and he fell to the dirty cobbles. As Morville made to kick him, the townsfolk rushed forward as one; the crowd becoming a mob.

FitzUrse grabbed his friend, pushed him to his horse and the four galloped to the castle, ignoring the pedestrians who fled from their path.

'Come on, Helwise,' William urged, spurring his own courser into a gallop.

Helwise screamed as a stone glanced off her skull, and William wheeled around, putting himself between his sister and the people gathered about the prone body of Robert Flower.

Screven placed himself on his mistress's other side as they galloped to safety.

Helwise took a last look around before the portcullis clanged down and the drawbridge over the ditch rose, relieved to see a dazed Robert Flower sit up just before he was lost to sight.

William reached up to help his sister dismount. 'Are you hurt?'

Helwise shook her head, then grimaced at the pain. She put her hands to her skull, then looked at her reddened fingers.

'Come, I'll help you to your bedchamber,' William said. 'Where is your husband?' he added, his face colouring with fury. 'He has not even paused to see if you are safe.'

'What do you expect?' Helwise asked. 'He has concerns only for himself.'

After a short silence, William said, 'I am sorry, Sister, you must prepare yourself. If Cnaresburg has reacted with this fury, the rest of Christendom must feel the same. I fear your husband will be present here for some time.'

Helwise said nothing.

'I shall stay here with you as much as I am able,' William added. 'I will not leave you alone with these men.'

Helwise nodded, then grimaced again. 'My thanks, Brother, your company will be most welcome.'

William glanced at the door to the hall at the bottom of the keep, then helped his sister up the narrow stone stairs to the bedchambers. The sound of the night's anger carried clearly up the steep round stairwell and his heart sank. Difficult times lay ahead.

Chapter 18

At first glance around the great hall, nothing seemed amiss. Fires blazed in the three large fireplaces. The candles of the chandeliers and candelabra flickered with flame, adding to the uplifting spirit of celebration.

Morville and Helwise sat at the centre of the lord's table with the knights and lords, from Sir Reginald FitzUrse to Nigel de Plumton, arranged to either side in order of status – other than William de Stoteville, who had ensured that he sat beside his sister in defiance of the higher titles of FitzUrse and Tracy. Lesser nobles, such as Pulleine of Fewston and Bilton from Hampsthwaite, sat at the centre of the low tables along with Thomas de Screven and other important local men, the richest merchants, and the parish priest. The rest of the available seats were occupied by the various vassals and men-at-arms of the gathered nobles.

Music was provided by a flautist, and tuneless but well-wetted voices grew louder and merrier with each jug of wine or ale.

Morville glanced around the gathered throng once more. There was no sign of William de Percy or any of his men. Morville grimaced in annoyance. Not only had Percy insulted him earlier by taking the mort, then issuing no invitation to feast at Spofford Manor – whilst Percy insisted on calling it a castle it was in reality no more than a large manor house, but Percy – one of King Henry's favourites – had not deigned to join the knights for the feast of venison; an unforgiveable insult.

Meat was a rarity – banned by the Church on Wednesdays, Fridays and Saturdays – and with Lent imminent a feast such as this night's was something to savour. Yet it was all ruined. Not only by the events of the afternoon and Percy's absence, but each course was slow in being brought to the table, and the larks, one of which he had just demolished, had been cold long before they had been placed before him and his guests. He threw the small bones on to the table in disgust and shouted for his steward, Jack.

Helwise stared at the half-eaten bird – one of the many caught by herself and the merlin – a feat of which she was proud with such a young bird accompanying a full hunt for the first time. A pity about the incident with her husband . . . She glanced at him as she remembered his near panic when he'd felt those talons at his head. True, the bird could have had his eye out, but it was the highlight of Helwise's day.

Morville caught her glance and smile, and scowled. She looked away and fell into conversation with her brother, sitting to her left.

'Is there any news of young Robert?'

He shrugged. 'The boy is fine, although a little dazed still. And recounting his narrow escape from Becket's murderers with some zeal.'

'Enough!' Morville roared, slamming his fist on the table. 'Do not mention that boy's name in this castle! And never, ever, refer to myself or my fellow lords as murderers, or you shall drive me to commit that very crime. Do you understand me?'

Stoteville lowered his head in acquiescence while a terrified Helwise grabbed his hand under the table.

Morville stared at his brother-in-law a moment longer then took hold of his wife's chin, tilting her head and pushing her hair and fillet away from her forehead to expose the now ugly bruise and gash on her pale skin. 'That is what those rogues did – to their lady! The lady who cares for their troubles, feeds the poorest and most wretched, and advocates for their needs. This is what they did!' He thrust Helwise's face away, ignoring her cry of pain and the tears that had escaped her lashes.

'You are hurting her, My Lord,' William de Stoteville said, his tone low and calm.

Morville stared at him a moment and let go of his wife's face. 'Steward!' he roared. 'Where in Christ's name is the venison?'

Jack leaned forward to speak in his lord's ear. 'Begging your pardon, My Lord. Many of the cooks and servers were at the market today. Not many have returned to the castle.'

Morville stared at him. 'Ensure that they are replaced forthwith,' he eventually said. 'And bring out that bloody venison.'

'Yes, My Lord,' the servant said, bowing and taking the half-full platters of leftover pork and skylark down to the lower tables to be gnawed over.

The venison arrived half a dozen goblets of wine later. Morville was morose, FitzUrse and Tracy loud and belligerent – mainly with each other, to the relief of everyone else present – whilst Brett gazed around him with unfocused eyes and a vague smile.

Nobody spoke to Morville, FitzUrse, Tracy and Brett except Morville, FitzUrse, Tracy and Brett, and the only ones who noticed were Helwise and William de Stoteville. Stoteville caught the eye of his vassal, Nigel de Plumton, Lord of the Manor of Plumton, who looked worried. Stoteville would have given anything to hear the opinions and words of his peers, but was reluctant to leave his sister's side when her husband was in such foul spirits.

She leaned into him, knowing her brother well enough to guess where his mind had turned. 'Go and join them,' she whispered. 'With my husband so hated, we must strain to retain good relations with our friends.'

William nodded and moved to stand but was stilled by Morville's roar.

'Hated? How dare you speak of your husband as such?'

The chatter and music silenced and the entire room of near two hundred souls stared at their lord and lady. Helwise wisely said nothing, knowing any attempt at appeasement would result in more ire.

'Am I not your friend, wife?' Morville asked.

Helwise nodded.

'Then do not betray me.' The words were uttered calmly, so calmly that Helwise only understood them when her husband's fist connected with her cheekbone and she fell, screaming from both the pain at the blow, plus fear at the crack she heard on its impact.

William stayed silent, but pulled his dagger as he climbed on to the bench and threw his entire weight at his brother-in-law.

Helwise crawled to safety as the other knights jumped to their feet. FitzUrse, Tracy and Brett attempted to heave Stoteville away from Morville, and the local nobles tried to heave FitzUrse, Tracy and Brett away from Stoteville.

Soon the entire hall was at odds with each knight's men fighting their master's rival's men. Staring at the carnage, Helwise was reminded of hunting hounds fighting over a kill. She alone witnessed William de Percy, favourite of King Henry, enter the hall, stare around him in contempt, then abruptly turn, his scarlet cloak swirling, to leave the troublesome knights to their brawl.

Chapter 19

11ᵗʰ July 2015

'Dan, no, I have a headache.' Sarah wasn't quite sure if she'd spoken the words aloud, she was still more in sleep than out of it, and Dan didn't stop. He rolled her unresponsive body on to her back and her entire focus was on keeping her legs together.

He persisted. There was no sensuous touching, no loving caresses, just fingers between her legs, trying to force them apart and gain access.

Sarah forced herself awake to again grunt, 'No,' then rolled back on to her front. She despaired when she felt those same fingers still seeking the depths of her body. She held her legs together, determined not to be used like this.

She tumbled back into dreams, thinking she was safe, then jerked awake as she was intimately touched.

'No, Dan, stop, let me sleep,' she mumbled, curling up into a ball.

'Oh come on, Sarah, it's been ages,' Dan said and smacked her backside.

Sarah started awake – properly now – sat up, and pulled both covers and legs up.

'What the hell's wrong with you, Sarah? I thought we were doing better lately.'

'I'm not against a little morning glory, Dan, but I was asleep and woke to you mauling me. I feel like a piece of meat.'

'Is it so wrong for a husband to desire his wife?'

'Of course not, if the husband takes the time to turn his wife on, so that she wants it too, rather than just taking what he fancies.'

'You make it sound like rape!'

'Well, to be honest, waking up like that kind of feels like rape.'

'But you're my wife!'

'Yes, and I love making love with you. But not when I'm asleep!'

'You bitch. You *are* shagging Mike, aren't you?'

'Oh my God.' Sarah rested her head in her hands. 'For the last time, I am not having an affair with Mike. I wouldn't do that to you.'

'How can I believe that? You don't even want to have sex with me any more.'

'Of course I do, I'd just like to be an active participant, that's all!'

'There you go again with the rape accusation.'

'I didn't say that, you did.'

'But how can a man trying to have sex with his wife be rape?'

'Are you kidding me? What, are you living in the Middle Ages now? You do not have an automatic right to my body. It's *my* body. And if I want to say no, then you respect that.'

'You *are* sleeping with Mike, aren't you?'

Sarah stared dumbfounded at her husband. How many times could she deny an accusation without foundation? 'No, Dan, I'm not,' she said, weary.

'Then who?'

'No one. And unless you can trust me, not you.'

'Fucking bitch!' He bent over her as she lay whimpering in their bed. 'Going off sex is the first sign of cheating,' he hissed in her ear. 'I know you're being untrue. I know it.'

He jerked back and stormed naked out of the room, fists

clenched. Sarah stared after him, knowing she'd had enough and wondering how she could separate their lives in a divorce. And where the hell could she go?

'Hi Helen,' Sarah said as Helen stood to embrace her friend.

'How are you?' Helen asked. 'I've been worried about you.'

The women both sat and Sarah shook her head. 'I don't know what's got into Dan lately. He was jealous after that love scene with Mike in the last play, but nothing like this, it's exploding out of him now.'

'Exploding? What do you mean? Has he hit you?'

'Oh no, no,' Sarah shook her head, then paused. 'Not yet. No more than the slap he gave me in the pub the other week, anyway.'

'Not yet?'

'No. No, sorry, I'm being silly. I didn't sleep well. There is no yet. Dan isn't like that.'

'He did a damned good impression in the Bailiff,' Helen pointed out.

Sarah stayed silent for a moment, then said, 'I'm going to the bar, what would you like?'

'No, I'll get them, you need a bit of TLC.' Helen reached across the table and squeezed her friend's hand, aware that Sarah's eyes were glistening.

'Large dry white wine, please. Thanks Helen.'

'Anytime.' Helen stood then sat back down. 'You know if it gets too much and you need some space, you're very welcome to stay with me.'

'Thanks, but things aren't that bad. He's my husband and he's clearly going through something. You know what men are like, he'll tell me what's going on eventually.'

'Yes, when it's all sorted.' Helen laughed, then went to the bar.

'I got a bottle,' Helen said, and stepped aside for the barman to put it and two glasses on the table. There were some advantages at least to having a broken wrist. 'I have a feeling this is going to be a long lunch.'

Sarah laughed. 'You know me so well.' She picked up the bottle and poured two large glasses, while Helen sat down.

'He does like you, you know.'

'Who, Dan?'

'No, Sarah. Mike.'

'Well, we're friends.'

'He likes you more than that and you know it.'

'Oh don't be silly.'

'I'm not, it's obvious to everyone – except you it seems.'

Sarah said nothing but looked thoughtful.

'Oh, you like him too, don't you?'

'Helen, no, I'm married with two kids.'

'So? I'm not asking if you're sleeping with him, just if you fancy him.'

'Helen!'

'You still haven't answered the question. You do, don't you?'

'Well okay, he's sweet.'

'Sweet? Could you find a more insulting compliment?'

'It's a married women's compliment,' Sarah said with a grin, 'and all I'm giving.'

'Giving me, anyway,' Helen said, laughing.

'Giving anyone,' Sarah insisted. 'Mind you, I'm paying the price as if I were giving Mike more – might as well do the crime if I'm already doing the time. Cheers.' She raised her glass and took a large gulp while Helen spluttered over her own wine.

'I'm joking! Only joking!' Sarah said as they both descended into helpless giggles.

'Well, be careful who you tell that joke to, Sarah.'

'Only you.'

'That's good.' Helen was serious again. 'You know, I *am*

worried. Not only about you but the rest of the players too. If Dan's cracking, it could fracture the whole group.'

'Thanks.'

'Oh don't be like that, Sarah, you know I'm here for you.'

'Yes, of course, sorry Helen. I'm just tired. Sick and tired of my husband and my marriage.'

Helen leaned over again to squeeze her hand. 'Is it really that bad?'

Sarah looked at, eyes steady. 'Pretty much, yes. We've fought before, but this time I just don't have the energy to fix things.'

'You don't love him any more.'

'I didn't say that.'

'Yes, Sarah, you kind of did.'

Chapter 20

'Are you sure we can afford this, Charlie?' Helen said as Charlie got up to get another round in.

'Absolutely. We still have a large chunk of the grant money left. We deserve a celebration, and as treasurer I officially declare that we can afford to do it in style.'

'Okay, if you're sure.' Helen relaxed and beamed. 'I still can't quite believe that we got funding.'

'It's about time,' Charlie said. 'We've been operating on a budget for years. It feels good to earn before the doors even open.'

'Well, hurry up and get the drinks in then,' Helen said with a laugh.

'Yeah, get a move on, mate, we're dying of thirst here,' Paul said.

Charlie flicked two fingers at him, then went to the bar.

'Oh, bloody hell, that Catherine lass is here – no wonder he was so keen to get up for the next round,' Paul said. 'He's not beating me with this one, too.'

'Oh don't tell me you two have bet on a woman again,' Sarah said.

'It's just a bit of fun.'

'No it isn't, it's degrading. Why don't you try to be nice and – I don't know – talk to her?'

'Where's the fun in that?' Paul asked.

'Yes, you might win the bet that way, mate,' Mike said at the same time.

The others laughed at the comical impression of a light bulb illuminating that Paul was barely aware he'd done, before he hurried to the bar asking Charlie if he could give him a hand.

Sarah smiled at Mike, pleased he'd taken her part, then glanced at Dan as he slammed his empty glass on the table. 'Off for a piss,' he said and got to his feet, knocking the table, and staggered off in the direction of the gents.

'Is he okay?' Ed asked.

Sarah sighed. 'He's fine, just drunk. He's been drinking all day,' she said, her exasperation with her husband clear to her friends.

'How long has that been going on?' Alec asked.

Sarah shrugged.

'We should try and talk some sense into him,' Alec added.

'Won't do any good, even if you can get him when he's sober,' Sarah said.

'We have to do something,' Helen said and laid a gentle hand on her friend's arm. 'It's affecting his performance on stage – I won't let him ruin this for us.'

Sarah shrugged again. 'I don't know what to tell you. I don't know what to do,' she said, tears threatening.

'Shush, it's okay, love,' Mike said, putting his arm around her shoulders and pulling her close. 'We're all friends here, and we're here for you.'

Helen widened her eyes at Sarah in warning, but she either didn't see or she refused to see. She patted Mike's knee. 'Thanks, Mike.' She straightened before Dan came back. Mike reluctantly dropped his arm and gave her a small smile.

Helen froze. *Shit, he's in love with her,* she thought. *Oh shit, shit, shit. I didn't realise it was that bad.* Her thoughts were interrupted by Dan thumping back down in his seat.

'Have they got the drinks yet?' he said, peering at the bar in search of Paul and Charlie.

'Could be a while yet,' Ed said, turning and spotting them both talking to Catherine. 'Doesn't look like they've even ordered them.'

'Bloody amateurs,' Dan sneered and levered himself back to his feet to hurry up his mates. Ed, Alec, Helen, Sarah and Mike looked at each other in silence.

'He'll be okay,' Mike said, patting Sarah's back. 'He'll sort himself out and soon.'

'What if he doesn't?' Sarah said. 'What then?'

'Then we find someone else to play FitzUrse,' Helen said.

Sarah looked at her. 'That's not what I meant, Helen.'

'Sorry.' Helen flushed and looked at the table.

'I'll have a word with him,' Mike said.

'I don't think that's a good idea,' Alec said. 'Ed and I will do it.'

'Why?'

Alec didn't reply, but turned to Ed. 'You're up for that, aren't you?'

'Yeah sure, whatever I can do to help,' Ed said.

'Here you go, sorry about the delay,' Charlie said as he put two pints and a couple of gin and tonics on the table, followed by another four pints from Paul. Everyone held the table steady as Dan retook his seat – just in case – then the other two sat down.

'Took you bloody long enough,' Mike said.

'Ah, but it was worth it,' Paul said, holding up a scrap of paper with numbers scribbled on it. 'Pay up, Charlie.'

Charlie grumbled, but got his wallet out. 'Enjoy it while it lasts – I'll get the next bird, then you'll be giving me that tenner back.'

'When did you two get so callous?' Sarah asked, disgusted with her friends, then erupted into giggles as Catherine poured her drink over Paul's head and plucked the tenner out of Charlie's fingers.

'That'll pay for the drink I've just wasted,' she said. 'Grow up, boys.' She sashayed to the door, turned and gave Sarah a wink before she left.

'I bloody paid for that drink,' Paul shouted after her, to even more amusement from his friends.

'I'm off to clean up,' he said. He punched Charlie on the arm. 'We both had a lucky escape with that one.'

Charlie tried to retort, but could not form any recognisable words through his laughter. Eventually, holding his stomach, he managed to say, 'Priceless, bloody priceless, well worth a tenner. I think I'm in love.' He collapsed into helpless laughter again, infecting the whole table – including Dan.

When Paul returned to the table, still wet, but at least not quite as sticky, Helen couldn't resist. 'Now careful, guys, we're already barred from the Borough Bailiff, we don't want to get barred from here too. We'll be running out of pubs at this rate.' Even Paul managed to see the funny side.

'I'm off to the loo, will you let me out, Dan?' Sarah said once the giggles had subsided enough.

Exiting the ladies, she was surprised by Mike, who grabbed her arm and pulled her into a hug.

'Mike, what are you doing?'

'Shush,' he said. 'Don't worry, I just want to say, well, I know things aren't great with Dan at the moment . . .'

'Mike, this isn't the time, we're both pissed and if Dan sees us, he'll kick off big time.'

'No, it's okay, the boys are having a word with him, he didn't even see me leave the table.'

Sarah nodded. 'Okay.'

'Sarah, I just want to say . . .'

'Well hurry up and say it then.' She laughed to take away the sting of her words.

'I just want to say, if you're not happy, you know, with Dan, you don't have to stay.'

'Mike, he's my husband and the father of my children.'

'I know, I know, but if he's making you unhappy . . . oh, sod it,' he said, grabbed Sarah's head and kissed her, hard.

Sarah squeaked and tried to push Mike away, but as he persisted, she found her resistance wavering, replaced by tingles in her belly and a quickening of her pulse. As she melted into Mike's kiss, the tingling spread until she was kissing him back with the same intensity.

Mike pulled back to look into her eyes as she pushed away, horrified at the realisation of what she'd done.

'I can't, Mike. I can't, I'm married, that shouldn't have happened.'

She broke the contact between them and rushed back to the bar, her thoughts and feelings in such a whirl she didn't see Helen standing against the wall, watching.

Chapter 21

'I don't get this scene,' Dan said.

Helen sighed, paused a moment, then explained again. 'We're covering the major incidents between Henry II and Becket to understand how such a close friendship ended so brutally.'

'Yes, I know that, but you keep talking about Clarendon – what the hell is Clarendon?'

'A palace near Salisbury,' Helen said, her teeth gritted. She took another breath to calm her irritation – she had explained this three times already, and her fears over Dan's mood and attitude were becoming reality. He was rude and surly to everyone – not just Sarah and Mike.

Helen just stopped herself from glancing at the pair of them – they were giggling like teenagers. She kept her attention on Dan. *Thank God I cast him as FitzUrse*, she thought – not for the first time – *at least this attitude suits The Bear perfectly.*

'Henry has called a council to meet at Clarendon Palace. He wants Becket and the bishops to make an oath that Henry has final authority in all things – including the sentencing of crimonious clerics.'

'Crimonious clerics?'

'Priests and monks who have broken the law.'

'But what's all the fuss about, surely the Church can sort them out?'

'No – they can only fine and defrock. Not a fitting punishment for robbery, rape or murder.'

'Huh. Fair enough. So what's Becket's problem?'

'Becket isn't popular with the English clergy – he wasn't even an ordained priest when Henry made him archbishop, remember – they don't trust him and he's trying to prove he's on their side. Henry is simply asking for too much.'

'Doesn't sound like it to me,' Dan said.

'Oh for God's sake, Dan,' Paul said, his patience running out. 'Can we just get on with the scene?'

'I don't understand why I'm in it,' Dan replied. 'How do we know it was our knights who were there?'

'We don't,' Helen said, all attempts at relaxed conversation now abandoned. 'We know Morville was there, the rest is dramatic licence.'

Dan opened his mouth but Paul interrupted before he could speak. 'Enough of this nonsense.' He paused in the shock of silence – Paul was usually mild mannered. 'Sorry guys, but seriously, we're here to rehearse. Let's just run through the scene, then we can talk it through later in the pub.'

'Okay everybody, positions please,' Helen called.

'Charlie, you as Becket centre stage. Ed and Sarah join him, you're bishops for this scene – Ed you're the Archbishop of York Roger de Pont l'Évêque, Sarah you're taking the role of Bishop Gilbert Foliot. Dan and Mike, I need you in the wings, with Paul as Henry behind you,' Helen instructed. 'From the top,' she said when everybody was in place.

Henry's voice reverberated from offstage. 'Get in there and force those damnable priests to submit. I'll castrate or execute any damned cleric who defies me!'

The bishops glanced at each other, clearly terrified.

'Calm yourselves,' Becket said. 'The King can be . . . dramatic at times. 'Tis an idle threat, purely for show.'

The bishops relaxed, though only a little – they had been

locked in this room for the past two days. But their archbishop knew their king better than any other man in Christendom. They had to trust him. To be fair, they had no other choice. The oath that King Henry demanded of them was too great; they were more than happy to leave the awkward and potentially life-threatening negotiations to the unwanted primary legate the King had forced upon them.

As one, they shrieked and retreated as Morville and FitzUrse burst through the door, flung away their cloaks to reveal their coats of mail, and unsheathed their broadswords.

'Definitely dramatic,' squeaked Roger de Pont l'Évêque, cowering away from the armed knights and clutching the arm of Gilbert Foliot.

'Submit in the name of the King,' Morville shouted.

'He has had enough of vacillating!' FitzUrse yelled into the face of Becket. The Archbishop stood his ground, but words failed him, for the moment at least.

'This is unacceptable.' L'Évêque stepped forward, only to retreat as Morville and FitzUrse turned their attention to him.

'Put down thy swords,' Becket quietly commanded. 'We are men of God and unarmed. Should the King wish to talk, we shall converse, but there is no need for this.'

'The King,' FitzUrse shouted, 'wishes agreement to his demands. Refusal of such is treason. And we do not countenance traitors.'

'My Lord, please, we are no traitors here – merely servants of God and the Church.'

'And the King!' FitzUrse shouted, brandishing his sword at Becket.

Becket studied the faces of the two men threatening him and realised he had no choice. 'Very well, I consent to the demand of my king. Please, sheathe your arms and allow the King and myself to discuss my oath.'

*

'Fabulous,' Helen cried. 'Even without costumes, it felt like the characters speaking. Well done!'

'Pub?' Mike said.

Chapter 22

29th March 1171

'It is good to be outside the curtain walls again,' said Richard le Brett, turning his face up to the sun.

'And out of the chapel,' FitzUrse growled.

The four knights had spent a particularly pious Lent, hearing Mass twice daily. On Easter Sunday – yesterday – they had donated the best cuts of meat in Morville's kitchen for the townsfolk to enjoy. Today was their first opportunity to hunt since Lent had begun, and the knights of Cnaresburg Castle intended to make the most of it.

Nigel de Plumton had joined them at the behest of Sir William de Stoteville, but William de Percy was once again absent, as were Sir John de Goldesburgh and Gamellor. Helwise had also elected to abstain from the day's activities.

Despite their reduced numbers, the men were determined to enjoy themselves and had elected boar as their quarry. The kill would not be as prestigious as the white hart they had brought down on their last outing, but it promised to be better sport. Boar could be dangerous and would test all of their wits, and hopefully lift their spirits. Relations between the men were tense after their confinement and the constant fights.

'I had the pleasure of dining with William de Percy at Spofford yesterday, William,' Nigel de Plumton said at length, while they waited for Morville and the others.

'Easter Sunday?' William de Stoteville asked.

Plumton nodded. 'It was a prestigious affair. Hamlin Plantagenet was in attendance, as well as William de Courcy, Lord of Harewood.'

'King Henry?'

Plumton shook his head. 'No, he dare not leave Normandy until he has heard from Pope Alexander.'

'He *dare* not? That does not sound like the King.'

'There is a great fear of excommunication.'

'I see. Is that why Percy did not invite us to Spofford for Easter?'

'Yes, I fear it is true. If Henry's messenger did not meet the Pope first, your brother-in-law and his cronies may be facing great trials ahead.'

'And my sister,' William muttered, watching an argument develop between Morville and FitzUrse over the courser The Bear had been given to ride. 'What was the tone of your dinner?'

'Sombre,' Plumton said. 'I owe you much, William, and must warn you. If the Church condemns them,' he nodded towards Morville and the other knights, 'they will find no support amongst the barons.'

Excommunication was the harshest punishment the Church could inflict on a man, and William nodded at the implications of Plumton's statement.

'That puts you in a delicate position, William.'

'Yes, it does indeed. I have no love for Morville, but I cannot abandon my sister to whatever fate befalls *him*.'

The men paused to watch Tracy and Brett physically restrain FitzUrse, whilst Morville, with his newly bruised jaw, was attended to by Mauclerk and Thomas de Screven.

'There may yet be no problem,' William said, his disdain evident on his face. 'They are likely to kill each other before Pope Alexander's judgement reaches their ears.'

Morville shook off his man and rushed FitzUrse. Tracy forward, receiving a violent shove for his trouble and Morville and The Bear rolled in the mud like street urchins, whilst Brett backed up out of their way. Neither Plumton nor Stoteville made any move to intervene, and Henry Goodricke, Cnaresburg's bailiff, walked up to join them.

'I like the idea of this hunt less and less,' he said. The other two nodded.

'We need to make our allegiance plain,' Plumton said. 'William de Courcy is holding a tournament at Harewood Castle next week. We should attend, and fight under the red and gold of King Henry, make sure they know whose side we are on.'

William and Henry nodded their agreement, but before either could say more, Richard le Brett spoke.

'A tournament at Harewood? God's blood, that's just what we need – we've been cooped up in this damned place for too long.'

The three lesser nobles looked at each other in dismay as Brett strode over to the squabbling knights.

'Stop that, save it for the tournament next week – at Harewood Castle!'

'What's that?' FitzUrse got to his feet and gave Morville a withering glare that stopped his next attack before it began. 'A tournament? Hugh, William, did you hear young Richard? A tournament, by God, there couldn't be better news. I for one am sick of the rain, the sights and the smells of this damnable town. A knights' tourney at Harewood? A hundred marks to the best placed of us. Who shall take the bet?'

All three took him up on it, their dispute forgotten.

Plumton, Goodricke and Stoteville stared at each other.

'They were not supposed to know about it,' Plumton whispered.

'Don't fret, Nigel, they were likely to hear a loose word from a groom or serving girl. But we shall make our own way there, we shall not travel with Morville and the other assassins.'

'Agreed,' Plumton and Goodricke said. 'Agreed.'

Morville led the hunting party into the marketplace, glancing warily around him as he did so. A complement of men-at-arms accompanied the nobles – a larger quota than Morville had ever needed before in Cnaresburg, but the townsfolk offered no threat. They simply and silently turned their backs as the knights rode past.

'Hugh,' Stoteville said, pointing down a narrow alley as they emerged on to the muddy high street.

Morville peered into the gloom, then quickly drew back his head as the smell of the rotting heap of meat struck him. It was the Easter meat the knights had foregone and given to the peasants and villeins.

'Even the bloody dogs don't want our food,' Morville growled, both angry and hurt at the dishonour shown him. The other knights were close behind and grumbled at the waste.

'Á Morville,' FitzUrse shouted, the battle cry a warning to all present. Then he laughed. Loudly.

'Shut up, you fool,' Stoteville said, pulling his courser up and turning to face the man.

FitzUrse's colour rose until his face was nearly as red as the cloak he wore.

'You do not speak to me like that, boy.'

'Then do no more to antagonise this town,' Stoteville replied, equally angry. 'These are *my* people. My family has lived amongst them since they arrived on these shores with King William.'

FitzUrse made to reply, but Morville intervened. 'Stop it, both of you.' He glanced behind FitzUrse at Tracy and Brett, then beyond them. The knights turned in their saddles to see the way behind blocked. Judging by the tools the men carried, peasants, villeins, butchers and more had gathered together to stand against the man they called lord.

The knights and men-at-arms positioned themselves to meet an attack, riding abreast boot-to-boot, and brought their boar spears to bear.

As one the townsfolk dropped the tools of their trades and turned their backs.

'They're pretending to be Becket,' Stoteville said with a glance at Morville. 'Non-threatening and unarmed.'

Morville ignored him, stared at the wall of backs before him, then yanked his courser's head around, kicked, and galloped towards Haya Park.

The other nobles glanced at each other, then followed. William de Stoteville brought up the rear with Plumton and Goodricke, at a walk, noticing how worried both Tracy and Brett looked as they continually glanced behind.

The three local men said nothing as they walked their mounts on, each of them lost in their own thoughts.

Chapter 23

April 1171

'Harewood Castle is at the top of this hill,' Morville said for the benefit of FitzUrse, Tracy and Brett, 'the other side of that wood.'

Nobody acknowledged him. They were all exhausted by the early start and seven-league trek, although it was the palfreys they rode that had done all the work.

Morville glanced behind him and grimaced at the state of his fellow knights; too much indulgence the night before a tournament never boded well, but there was no stopping Tracy and FitzUrse when they had the taste of wine in their gullets. And Brett was just as bad, as was Morville himself. Morville laughed out loud at the truth of it, to the consternation of his mount, which shied at the sudden noise. But it was no surprise that they took to the table and their cups quicker and more enthusiastically these days.

There had been no further word from King Henry since Hamelin Plantagenet's 'welcome' at Cnaresburg in January, and it was becoming apparent that his favourites – not only Plantagenet, but Courcy and Percy in particular – were keeping their distance. Even Goldesburgh, Plumton and Goodricke were more often staying away, and he was well aware of Stoteville's view. Though the two of them had never been friends, they had tolerated each other since Morville's marriage to Helwise; the marriage which had brought Morville a castle, the Stoteville's titles, and was an excellent match.

Morville glanced back again, this time at the destriers, the warhorses the knights would ride at the tournament. A risk to bring such fine beasts, but Morville at least recognised they were sorely in need of friends, and if the sacrifice of a destrier in ransom bought them a friend or two, it would be well worth the loss of horseflesh. That was relatively easy to replace.

The cart with their armour and weapons lagged behind, the two packhorses barely able to drag it up the steep hill, but Thomas de Screven and Hugh Mauclerk were in attendance and would ensure that their belongings did not fall too far behind.

'Ah, it feels like civilisation again,' Tracy said with a broad grin at the sight of knightly entourages approaching the gates of Harewood Castle from three separate directions. 'It is good to be in the company of knights rather than peasants.'

'And what in God's name do you think we are?' FitzUrse demanded.

'Calm yourself, Reginald, I was including you in my observation. Is it not good to gaze on colour and riches rather than dirt and poverty?'

FitzUrse grunted, his temper calming, and a rare smile was just discernible behind the hair of his full beard. 'Is that not Stoteville and Plumton?'

'Yes, it is indeed,' Morville said. 'Goldesburgh too, even Gamellor.'

'Why did they not ride with us?' Tracy asked, his voice petulant.

'There's far more prestige in accompanying William de Percy, it appears,' Morville said nodding at the blue and yellow livery of the men-at-arms.

'More prestige?' FitzUrse growled. 'Shame on them. We're the only men with enough courage to have cut out the canker of England!'

Morville said nothing, and noticed that Tracy looked worried. Very worried. Maybe the drunken sot had some sense in his head after all, not that it would do him much good if he persisted in toadying to Reginald FitzUrse.

It escaped none of the knights' attention that not a single greeting was passed their way, but as one they all chose to ignore the fact.

'William,' Morville greeted his brother-in-law. 'I did not know you would be attending.'

'Hugh! What are you doing here?'

'That's a fine way to greet your sister's husband, why would I not be here?' Morville said, knowing full well that Stoteville had been aware of his intentions to attend.

'Well, with the Church's attitude to tournaments, I assumed you would not risk antagonising them further.'

'I do not answer to the Church, William, only the King.'

William de Stoteville nodded. 'Begging your pardon, My Lord.'

Morville changed the subject. 'It seems Courcy has attracted a good turnout.'

'Yes, Henry is more confident in the Church's favour after events just past – it has been a very quiet few months, more than time enough to tourney.'

'Most of the barons and knights of England have made the journey,' Morville remarked, glancing around at the garish colours declaring the wealth and status of their wearers; or their wearers' masters.

'There has been scant opportunity to win coin or settle old scores this year,' Stoteville said then added sotto voce, 'Mandeville is here. Beware him, Hugh, he was furious that you reached Becket before him and has been disclaiming your name to anyone with an ear.'

'What? Because he was tardy and we accomplished the task in his stead?'

Stoteville grimaced but stilled the retort ready on his tongue.

'He will have to beware me should I spot him in the mêlée,' Morville continued, oblivious to Stoteville's reaction.

'There will be no mêlée, Hugh, it is a joust of peace – the quintain and ring.'

'What? By the name of all that is holy, why?'

'Henry does not wish to antagonise Pope Alexander further. No swordplay and no mêlée. Courcy did well to obtain permission for this only.'

'God's blood, what is a tourney without swords or mêlée? Where's the opportunity for ransom?'

'There is none, the knights entering the joust are required to pay a fee. The best man will take the purse.'

'But where's the fun in that?' Morville asked.

Stoteville glanced at him in frustration. If the oaf could not recognise the enmity in the glares of the gallant knights, and realise they all suffered the consequences of his and his cronies' actions that fateful night, Stoteville would not be the one to enlighten him.

Chapter 24

The heralds' trumpets silenced the crowd of nobles and men-at-arms, and every man turned their attention to the lists.

'Earls, Barons, Knights, Gentlemen. Sir William de Courcy, Lord of Harewood, bids thee welcome at Harewood Castle,' Courcy's pursuivant-of-arms announced as the trumpet notes faded, 'for a celebration of the joust.'

The knights roared approval and FitzUrse turned to Tracy and said, 'Though we are not per se jousting.'

'No, indeed, a mere practice,' Tracy said.

'Although it is good to be away from Cnaresburg, even if only for a day or two,' Brett said. Morville glanced sharply at him, but his words were drowned out by another blast of trumpeted notes.

'Bid thee welcome to Sir Hamelin Plantagenet, Earl of Surrey. Most esteemed guest of honour, and our first contender!'

The gathered noblemen and their entourages burst into tremendous applause and cheers, each plying further admiration for the King's brother, despite the fact that his entire head was enclosed by the steel of his modern helm and he was essentially deafened.

Although Plantagenet's opponent was a mere quintain, he rode into the lists in full armour: padded gambeson; mail coat, hood and even legs; spurs attached to his boots, and heavy lance held erect.

He circled the field, then guided his destrier to the head of the lists. A wooden rail ran down the centre of the field, and a blue shield adorned with the golden fleur-de-lis of Louis VII was mounted on a crossbar attached to a ten-foot pole.

He flicked his visor closed: an act of affectation as he faced no opponent, but the gathered nobles got the message nonetheless. Plantagenet would do this virtually blind, no man could beat him.

Plantagenet kicked his horse, who strode straight into a canter, then a gallop. He levelled his lance, balancing it on his thigh, and aimed it at the quintain dead ahead. He leaned back to adjust his aim and struck it squarely. The shield sprung back, allowing the Earl safe passage.

He pulled his mare up, wheeled around and circled the field, delighting in the applause as the quintain was reset.

'Will he not attempt the ring next?' Brett asked, confused.

'No,' Morville replied. 'Each man will have three tries at the quintain today, three attempts at the ring tomorrow, then the best of them will strike at both the day after.'

They looked up as Plantagenet took a second turn at the quintain, a glancing blow not as true, but the quintain swung away nonetheless. The applause was just as raucous. The King's brother could fall and still be heralded, at least in public, as champion.

His third attempt was as clean as his first and he lifted his visor, stood in his stirrups, and thumped his chest in triumph as he completed his final lap of honour.

'We're losing the light,' FitzUrse said. 'We have not been called yet, it will soon be dark.'

'Maybe that's the idea,' Morville said, then looked up as his name was called. 'Damn them, they give me no warning? Mauclerk! Bring my horse, now!'

Brett helped him into his mail, he grabbed his helmet – of the older and most common design: conical with only a nose guard to protect his face – and hurried to the entrance to the lists, accompanied by the impatient slow handclap of the waiting nobles.

Flustered, Morville grabbed the reins from Mauclerk and lifted his foot, ready for his clerk to clamp his hands together and heave him into the saddle.

Morville took a deep breath to steady himself. He scanned the silent crowd, then tapped his helmet to ensure it was secure on his head. He was unnerved. He knew he had kept everyone waiting, through no fault of his own, but he had never known a cavalcade of knights be so quiet.

He took another breath, brought his lance to bear, and kicked his spurs into his horse's flanks. Shutting out the disapproval of his peers, he focused on the quintain, aimed, and hit it square. The wooden shield sprang back and he heaved on the reins to slow.

Morville glared at his silent audience, determined not to show his unease. One gaze in particular caught his attention. A priest, no doubt Harewood's parish priest, stood with arms crossed, his eyes full of a hate so malevolent, Morville had only seen the like on a battlefield.

Shaken, he turned his destrier's head and trotted back to the head of the lists for his next attempt.

Once again he pushed his helmet down hard on his head, took a calming breath and kicked. He leaned to his right in a last-minute adjustment of his lance, but was too late, his mind not on the task at hand. The ten-foot lance connected with the edge of the quintain, and the force of the blow was thrown back into his shoulder, knocking him off balance. The quintain stayed in place and his body connected with it at full gallop.

Winded, he allowed Mauclerk to help him to his feet, pulled off his helmet, then wished he hadn't as the crowd's cheers and catcalls penetrated through the ringing in his ears.

He limped away from the lists, head hanging as Brett chased down his horse and the pursuivant announced FitzUrse.

Sir Reginald FitzUrse, mounted, sat at the head of the lists and surveyed the crowd of silent barons, knights and assorted lords surrounding the jousting field.

He reached up to secure his helmet, then changed his mind and snatched it from his head and threw it to the turf. If they would force him to the lists at dusk, he would not hamper himself any further – no matter what Hamlin Plantagenet had done in full daylight.

Shutting out the mutterings of the gathered nobles, he brought his lance up, couched it against his shoulder and focused on the quintain. He could only just see it. No wonder Morville had missed.

He kicked his horse into action, adjusted his direction, and aimed. Dead centre.

He turned his horse into a lap of honour, but heard not a single cheer. His peers were silent.

He realised the futility of what he was doing, realised he could not win, and finally realised they held his recent deeds in abhorrence, no matter that the act had been instigated by their king.

He cast his eyes around the crowd in contempt, lingering on those of Hamlin Plantagenet as the man closest to Henry, then turned and cantered out of the lists.

Morville, Tracy and Brett were at the gates. With one gesture they followed him, back to Cnaresburg.

Chapter 25

'But how could they treat us so?' Tracy whined before emptying his goblet.

'Does this mean that the King has forsaken us?' Brett asked before any answer was given.

'How the damnation do I know?' FitzUrse said. 'We're cut off here, far from Normandy. Has Percy not said anything to you, Hugh?'

'Of course not, I would have told you should he have spoken to me. This turn of events is as much of a surprise to me as you.'

'But what shall we do?' Tracy said. 'We are naught without the favour of our king.'

'The Church must be holding sway over him,' Morville said.

'And you know Henry, he'll put himself above all others,' FitzUrse added.

'Indeed,' Morville said. 'If he is in such straits with the Pope, he would not hesitate to cast us aside.'

'So, we are on our own,' FitzUrse said.

'Yes, we are on our own – at least for the time being,' Morville said. 'If only you had stayed your hands and merely arrested Becket.'

'Hugh! You saw how hard I tried to talk sense into the man,' FitzUrse said. 'I was the only one who tried, if I recall. The rest of you scurried away like rats.'

'Yes, but what else could we have done?' Tracy said. 'We did all we could to persuade him.'

'You call slicing off the top of his head persuasion?' Morville said.

'I was only trying to help!' Brett said. 'Put him out of his misery.'

'Yes, but murder, Richard. Murder,' Tracy said, emptying another goblet and reaching for the flagon of Rhenish.

'He was a traitor,' Brett said. 'It was not murder but execution sanctioned by the King.'

'He did not order Becket's death, Richard,' Morville said.

'No, but he demanded vengeance,' Tracy said. 'He wanted the Archbishop silenced.'

'Well, we've done that all right,' FitzUrse said. 'We've resolved his problem, and now he abandons us. What reward is that for his most loyal knights?'

'No reward,' said Brett, 'but vilification and shunning.'

'Have a care, Richard, your talk is nearing sedition,' Morville said.

'I was just saying.'

'The point is,' FitzUrse said, 'what do we do about it?'

'What can we do?' Tracy asked. 'Without the King's favour, we are doomed.'

'William, that's putting it a bit strongly,' Brett said. 'Why don't we just stay here until Becket is forgotten?'

'That could take a lifetime,' Tracy said.

'I'm only trying to help,' Brett said. 'Would you pass that flagon or have you drunk it all?'

Tracy slammed his goblet on the scarred wood of the table. 'And what if I have? Hugh has plenty more in his cellar.'

'Speaking of more,' Morville said, 'where the blazes is my steward? We've been sitting here a half-hour and have no repast.' He stood and strode to the door, then roared for Jack. When no server was forthcoming, he roared instead for his wife.

'Helwise, what the devil is going on?' he said when she arrived.

Flustered, the long sleeves of her bliaut whipped around her knees. 'There's illness in the town, My Lord,' she said. 'They believe it punishment from God.'

'Punishment? What the devil for? What have they done?'

'Harboured you,' Helwise said, staring at her husband, her face expressionless. Morville said nothing, although his mouth worked frantically.

'They have heard word of your reception at Harewood Castle, My Lord. They believe you against the Church *and* against the King,' Helwise continued.

'The ungrateful buggers,' FitzUrse said, and Morville spun round. All the knights had congregated behind him. 'We ridded the King and his kingdom of a serious threat. The Young King is now safe, thanks to us. And this is how we are repaid?'

Morville recovered his composure. 'And what of the garrison?' His blood ran cold at the thought that his men-at-arms may have also absconded.

'Still present, My Lord,' Mauclerk said, stepping out of the shadows. 'The castle is still strong.'

'Blacksmith? Marshal?'

'The marshal is yet here, although minus a couple of grooms. The smith . . . the smith was persuaded to stay.'

'Persuaded? By you?'

Mauclerk nodded.

'Good man. Keep a close eye on him, and ensure the blades and crossbow quarrels he crafts are of strength and high standard.'

'Of course, My Lord.'

'And go to the sergeant-at-arms, have him put his best cooks in my kitchen. You can bring us wine. My Lords, please, return to the table. We are in need of a plan of action.'

Chapter 26

Tracy lunged forward, swinging his sword. FitzUrse blocked his thrust, continued the arc of his parry, then reversed direction, aiming for Tracy's head. Tracy ducked, then caught FitzUrse's mailed wrist with his blade.

FitzUrse stepped to the left to keep his balance, prepared to strike, and this time connected with Tracy's helmet.

Both men stepped back to regain their breath, then Tracy again swung low. Blocked by FitzUrse. Right to left, this time high. He grinned at the solid thunk of his sword striking FitzUrse's helmet, swung his sword back – knowing he was exposed and taking the gamble that FitzUrse would not yet have regained his wits from the ringing in his ears – and swung on a diagonal to catch FitzUrse's arm.

'That's five, my turn,' Morville said. FitzUrse had already initiated his answering blow and did not pull it, but caught Tracy's thigh.

Tracy fell, howling in pain and outrage. Not only had FitzUrse's turn in the practice circle ended, but Tracy was not wearing leg mail. Padded leather did little to soften the blow of a heavy sword strike, even that of a dulled practice blade.

'Reginald, enough!' Morville shouted.

FitzUrse took off his helmet and cupped his ear, feigning deafness, then reached out a gauntleted hand and hauled Tracy to his feet. Tracy glared at him but said naught, instead turning to face Morville.

Five strokes later, he turned to do the same with Brett then took his place in the circle as FitzUrse entered the centre and faced Morville.

Too soon, FitzUrse turned to Tracy, who had not yet recovered from his gruelling turn in the centre of the practice circle. FitzUrse seemed unaffected by his rounds with Morville and Brett, despite his heavy mail and padded gambeson on a warm spring day.

Tracy scowled at him, still smarting from the blow to his thigh, and stepped forward, lunging at his opponent, despite the convention that the man in the centre be the aggressor. FitzUrse grinned and countered, then launched a heavy and rapid sequence of thrusts, slices and strikes; once more sending Tracy to the ground.

'My turn,' Morville announced, stepping forward. FitzUrse spun round, adding momentum to his sword, which Morville only just managed to block. He struck back, but FitzUrse had anticipated his move, fended him off, then spun again to block Tracy's sword.

Both knights swung at The Bear, one sword glancing off FitzUrse's shoulder, barely registering with him. His face a mask of concentration and effort, his total awareness was captured by his sword.

As the three men turned, Brett stepped in alongside FitzUrse, then all four knights engaged in battle, the only sound the clash of sword against sword, mail and helmets, accompanied by grunts of exertion. Not one of them had strength enough for words.

Minutes later, all four backed away, resting their sword tips on the ground and leaning on the pommels, panting heavily.

Morville was the first to regain his composure. 'Enough for today.' The others nodded in relieved agreement and, as one, sat, dropping the swords and pulling off helmets. Morville gestured to Mauclerk, who hurried over with a large flagon and four goblets.

*

FitzUrse topped up Tracy's goblet then glanced at the southern curtain wall and tower. 'It's coming on well.'

'Yes,' Morville said. 'They should have it finished soon, then we'll be able to withstand any attack.'

'Do you really think it will come to that?' Brett asked.

'You witnessed our reception at Harewood,' FitzUrse said. 'If Henry has turned against us, there will be no shortage of volunteers to rid the kingdom of us.'

'Surely Henry hasn't turned against us in truth,' Morville said. 'We carried out his bidding.'

'Yes, but all it takes is one intemperate proclamation falling on the wrong ears,' FitzUrse said.

All four remained quiet, none of them daring to voice the concern that they themselves had acted on an 'intemperate proclamation' rather than a carefully considered order.

'Ah, the crossbows,' Morville said, breaking the uncomfortable silence. The others turned to see thirty men-at-arms approaching. 'Good, I want to see how true their aim is.'

'We should move,' said Brett, nodding in the other direction at the bales of straw being set up as targets. 'We are in the line of fire.'

Morville and FitzUrse glanced at each other, both wondering how true Brett's ill-considered words would prove to be.

Chapter 27

22nd July 2015

Helen saved her work and got up to answer the door with an audible curse. 'Why does someone always have to knock on the door when I'm in the zone and the words are flowing?'

'Oh thank goodness you're in, Helen,' Sarah said. 'It's so great you work from home.'

Helen opened her mouth to say, 'Yes, work being the point,' but changed her mind as she realised that Sarah was barely holding back tears. 'Come in, Sarah, what's wrong?'

Sarah didn't answer, but took off her hat and coat, then looked up at Helen and pushed her hair away from her face to reveal a purple bruise on her temple.

'He hit you?'

Sarah nodded and lost the control she'd been holding on to. Helen hugged her and led her to the sofa in the living room, her heart sinking.

'I'm sorry, Helen, I didn't mean to break down on you.'

'Don't be silly, Sarah, I'm your friend, you can always come to me if you're in trouble.'

'Th-th-thank you.'

Helen reached to the coffee table for a box of tissues and handed it to Sarah, who took a handful, mopped her face, and blew her nose.

'Feel better?'

Sarah nodded, but tears started to fall again. 'I'll be okay in a minute,' she said, taking a deep breath.

'I'll go put the kettle on, you could do with a cup of tea.'

'I could do with a bottle of wine,' Sarah said, with a shaky laugh.

'I can do that too,' Helen said. 'I'll just be a moment.'

'What happened?' Helen asked, back on the sofa, both women clutching glasses of Sauvignon.

'He laid into me about Mike, said I was getting too friendly and leading him on. Asked me *again* if we were sleeping together.'

'Are you?' Helen asked.

'No! Not you too – Helen, you know me better than that.'

'I saw you, Sarah, kissing him outside the ladies at the pub.'

Sarah buried her face in tissues again, then when Helen said nothing more, she took another gulp of wine.

'It was nothing, really. We've just been getting on so well lately and Dan and I have been going through a rough patch for what seems forever.'

'So you got a bit carried away.'

'Yes! That's it exactly.'

'Is that the only time it happened?'

Sarah looked down at her wine and emptied her glass.

'I guess that answers that question,' Helen said and refilled it.

'Anyway, back to Dan,' Sarah said. 'We were having a full-blown row – another one – when Mike called.'

'You answered it, didn't you?'

Sarah nodded. 'Dan said that it showed that Mike meant more to me than he does, and proved that we were sleeping together.'

'Then what happened?'

'I—'

'Sarah?'

'I denied it, but by this time I was so furious with him, I mean talk about double standards – I've lost count of the number of times I've caught him watching porn on his phone.'

'What did you say?'

'I said I wasn't but I wished I was. That I've had it with Dan's moods and aggression and told him that he couldn't control me any more and it would be his fault if I did get with Mike.'

'Oh Sarah.'

'And he hit me. So it's my own fault.'

'No. No Sarah, it's not your fault. Yes, you could have handled it better, but that's no excuse for him to punch you in the face!'

'I was shocked more than anything,' Sarah said, taking another sip. 'Dan's never been violent before.'

'But he has been getting more and more belligerent.'

'You've seen it too! Yes – ever since we started this play. It's like I don't know him any more. He's not the man I married.'

'And Mike? I know you've always been friendly, but not like this.'

'Yes, he's different too. He's there for me, and makes me laugh. He even listens.' Sarah gave a hollow laugh. 'Just like Dan used to.'

'So what now?'

'I can't go back there, I just can't.'

'No, of course you can't, and you're welcome to stay here, but what about the kids?'

Sarah rested her head on her hand and Helen rescued the glass of wine before the remainder slopped on to her sofa.

'What am I going to do?' Sarah wailed through sobs.

'John and Kate shouldn't be in the middle of this, Sarah.'

'I know.'

'Where's Dan now?'

'At work.'

'Right. Then we'll go and get your stuff, the sooner the better.'

'Thank you, Helen, but I don't want to impose – you don't

want me underfoot all day when you're working. I'll stay with Mike, he won't mind.'

Helen shut her eyes for a moment and took a deep breath, then said, 'Sarah, that's not a good idea. Running off to Mike will not help things – you can't throw away a ten-year marriage like that.'

'I'm not! Dan did that when he hit me!'

Helen nodded. 'But think of the kids – how would they handle it? And if Dan gets help, some counselling and anger management, maybe he can work out where this aggression is coming from and deal with it.'

'The way he is now, he won't even hear of it,' Sarah said.

'Okay, but still give it some time before shacking up with Mike.'

'Maybe you're right,' Sarah said and leaned forward to refill her glass. 'Thanks, Helen, you're a good friend.'

Helen clinked her own glass against Sarah's. 'Always.'

'I just don't know what's got into everyone.' Sarah said. 'It's not just Dan and Mike who have changed. Paul and Charlie are competing over everything. I know they always had a rivalry, the two of them always being up for the main parts, but it's gotten ridiculous. Do you know Charlie even took Catherine out to dinner?'

'The girl who threw her drink over Paul?'

'The very same. Paul's furious. He's getting so bossy as well – in the rehearsals it sounds as if he's the director these days. What's got into everybody?'

Helen hesitated. 'Nothing. I hope.'

The two women looked at each other and paled.

Chapter 28

'Thanks for coming, everyone – I appreciate the hours you're putting in,' Helen said.

Mike laughed. 'Not too hard to come to the pub for the evening.'

'Cheers to that!' Paul said, raising his glass in a toast.

'When did you start drinking wine?' Charlie asked.

'Just got sick of the beer, mate, fancied a glass of Rhenish.'

'A glass of what?'

Paul shrugged. 'Just fancied a change.'

'Anyway,' Helen said, a little uneasy, 'let's get down to business. I need an update on costumes, props and sets. Sarah, are John and Kate still on board to help?'

'Yes, I want to keep them busy, take their minds off things.'

'What things?' Alec asked.

Sarah took a deep breath. 'Dan and I have split.'

Silence.

'What did you say?' Paul asked, his voice measured and low.

'You heard her,' Mike said.

'Is this anything to do with you?'

'No. It's to do with me and Dan,' Sarah said quickly.

'Well, nice timing, Sarah. What the hell have you done that he won't join us?'

Sarah stared at him and pushed her hand through her hair to display the bruise faintly visible under her make-up. 'I've done nothing, the fault is his. And he's not here because he's in the

Borough Bailiff, getting pissed and chatting up the landlady.'

'I thought he was barred from there,' Alec said.

'It seems the landlady has a soft spot for him,' Sarah said, her voice pitched high.

'Shush, it's okay, Sarah.' Mike stroked her back to calm her.

'Yeah, I'm not surprised, looking at the two of you,' Paul said.

Sarah opened her mouth to retort but Helen spoke first. 'This isn't helping. Dan will come around, he just needs a bit of time. Alec, I know you're sound and lighting, but will you understudy Dan as well, just in case? At least he's only in the one major scene.'

'But if Alec plays FitzUrse, who will do the lighting in the final scene? It's the most complicated,' Ed said.

'I will,' Helen said. 'Alec will do all the programming ahead of time anyway and I can follow instructions. And it's only plan B. Dan's never let us down before. It will all come together on the night.'

'I bloody well hope so,' Paul grumbled. 'It's looking a bloody shambles at the minute.'

'All right, mate, calm down,' Charlie said. 'It sounds like Helen has everything under control.'

'Thanks, Charlie. Enough of Dan, where are we with the costumes, Sarah?'

'Costumes we're all right with. It's mainly tunics and hose, which are pretty simple to put together. I've bought *The Medieval Tailor* so have patterns for everything I need to make, and Kate's helping me.'

'That's great, Sarah, do you need any more help?' Helen asked.

'No, I'm fine for the moment – to be honest, it's good for me to keep busy.'

Helen nodded. 'Alec, Ed, where are we on the sets?'

'We have the main backdrop in a masonry design, and I think it will work if we then use different furniture to show the difference between castle, great hall and church,' Ed said.

'Good,' Helen said.

'We already have the basics, I'll use one of the tables as an altar, so just need an altar cloth and a cross.'

'We,' Alec said.

'What?'

'You said "I". It's "we" who are doing the props.'

'Yes, of course, that's what I meant.'

'Didn't say it though.'

'My sincere apologies, Alec. *We* will use one of the tables for an altar. Then *we* will keep an eye on the local auction house for a suitable chair that *we* can upholster to create a throne.'

'Good,' Helen said, trying to quell the unexpected animosity between the two men. 'What else do we need?'

'A crown for Paul,' Mike said. 'A crook, or whatever they're called, for Charlie, and parchment, quills and inkpots.'

'Did archbishops have crooks back then?' Ed asked.

'We need to check,' Helen said. 'Then there's mail coats and hoods, and those conical helmets with a nose guard for the knights.'

'And swords,' Mike put in.

'Okay, that all sounds a bit pricey,' Helen said.

'eBay is a good place to start,' Sarah suggested. 'Plenty of theatrical outfitters and LARP companies. I can have a look if you like.'

'Great, thanks Sarah,' Helen said. 'How much do we have to spend, Charlie?'

'What? Erm, not sure to be honest.'

'What do you mean you're not sure? You're the bloody treasurer,' Paul shouted, slamming his wine glass on to the table then cursing as the stem broke. 'Oh, for God's sake! Someone get me another wine.'

Mike jumped to his feet to go to the bar. 'Anyone else?'

Helen looked around the table and realised everyone was on wine. *When did we all start drinking wine?* she thought, the sinking feeling in her belly gathering depth. 'Here Mike,' she said, brandishing a £20 note. 'Get a couple of bottles.'

'That won't be enough.'

'Then add to it,' she snapped. 'Sorry, Mike, that's all I have. Anyone else?'

'It's okay, Helen, I've got it covered,' Mike said and rushed to the bar.

Helen took a deep breath, but Paul beat her to it.

'Charlie? You haven't answered my question. How much money is left?'

'I don't know, about fifty quid I think.'

'Fifty quid? How the hell is that all we have left from a £500 grant? We haven't bought the bloody props yet!'

'Well, we had that night out, I had to pay for the damage Dan did in the Bailiff, and there's the fees for hiring the theatre for the rehearsals . . .'

'So you've spent it,' Paul said.

'No, *we've* spent it,' Charlie said.

'Have you got the accounts?'

'Well, no, not really. The cash is in a jar in my kitchen and I reckon there's about fifty quid left, but I'll add it up and let you know.'

'Are you telling me you've not kept accounts?' Paul demanded.

'Well, yeah, I guess I am. No one's needed them before, so I've not bothered. Come on, mate, you can trust me.'

'Can we? You've spent over four hundred quid and don't have much to show for it. Are you sure the money's gone on this drama group?'

'Just what the hell are you accusing me of, *mate?*' Charlie spat the question and stood.

Paul rose to match him, braced his hands on the table, and

leaned over to push his face into his friend's. 'I think it's quite clear what I'm accusing you of, *mate.*'

'Guys, guys, stop it, what the hell are you doing?' Helen said, standing herself and putting her good arm between the men in an attempt to keep them apart. 'Charlie, can you put some figures together – some accounts?'

'Yes, sure, I'd have done it already if I knew you didn't trust me.'

'We do trust you, Charlie,' Helen, Sarah and Alec chorused.

'But I see the rest of you don't,' Charlie said.

'Shit, shit, shit, shit,' Helen said, slowly retaking her seat.

'What the hell's wrong with you, woman?' Paul demanded.

'It's not what's wrong with her, but what's wrong with the rest of us, isn't it, Helen?' Sarah said.

Helen nodded. 'We've got a big problem.'

'What? God's wounds, tell us!' Paul said.

Helen looked up at him sharply. 'Remember the spirit board?'

'Oh don't be bloody ridiculous.'

'She's not,' Sarah said. 'Look at us, we're all . . . different.'

'And what's just happened also happened between Henry and Becket – they fell out over Becket omitting to make accounts and Henry accused him of embezzlement,' Helen said. 'Don't you see? The spirit board worked – we brought them through.'

'Oh don't get hysterical,' Paul sneered. 'What the hell are you doing here anyway? This is the business of kings, begone, Saxon.' He looked around at everybody. 'What? It was a *joke.*'

Chapter 29

June 1171

'My Lord, horsemen approach,' Mauclerk said as he burst into the great hall.

'Who is it?' Morville demanded.

'They fly no banner, but one of the riders is Sir William de Percy.'

'Percy? I wonder what's brought him so low, that he graces us with his presence,' FitzUrse said.

'Should we unbar the gates?' Mauclerk asked, ignoring FitzUrse's scowl.

Morville hesitated. 'How many men does he have with him?'

'A company, near enough, perhaps fifty men or more.'

'So many?' Tracy asked, then turned to Morville. 'He's here to attack.'

Morville glanced at him then rose. 'I need to see them.' He hurried up the stairs to the top of the keep and peered out at the approaching men.

'Permit them entry,' he told Mauclerk.

'Hugh, do you think that's wise?'

'If he were here to attack, he would have more men and brought siege engines.'

'Yes, but it may be a trick,' Tracy said.

'Only one way to find out,' Morville said and led the way out to the courtyard to greet his guests. 'My Lord Percy, what brings you to Cnaresburg?'

Percy dismounted but said naught, instead gesturing to the other riders. Morville recognised Hamelin Plantagenet and William de Courcy then focused on the fourth man briefly before dropping to one knee. 'My Liege, welcome to Cnaresburg,' he said.

FitzUrse, Tracy and Brett knelt a fraction after Morville, with an audible gasp from Tracy.

Henry Plantagenet pulled his hood from his face. 'It is a dark day indeed when a king must ride through his own kingdom in secret lest he be recognised.'

'Welcome,' Morville said again. 'May I offer you some refreshment after your journey?'

'You may indeed,' Henry said, striding towards the keep and great hall within, without making any indication the knights could rise.

The four glanced at each other, then regained their feet the moment King Henry turned his back to them. Percy smirked at them, but Hamelin Plantagenet and Courcy's expressions remained unreadable.

'Hugh, where is Helwise?'

'William, I did not see you there, why did you not send word you were coming?'

Stoteville glared at him. 'The King did not wish it. Where is my sister?'

Morville shrugged. 'About somewhere – the mews perhaps, she seems to spend most of her time with the hawks these days.'

Glancing around the table filled with dishes of venison in wine sauce, stewed swan, beef pottage and a spicy Leche Lombard, amongst many other delicacies, Morville was satisfied he had provided a meal fit for his king, even if it was being served by men-at-arms rather than young, pretty and buxom girls. He noticed Henry glare at the men as they brought more rich fare to the table, then the King glanced at Morville, eyebrows raised.

Morville filled his king's goblet, unwilling to explain that his servants had deserted him. 'What brings you to Yorkshire, My Liege?'

'I am on my way to inspect my new mighty castle at Riche Mont, which perchance provides the perfect opportunity to speak to you.' He raised his goblet to include FitzUrse, Tracy and Brett.

'It is our very great pleasure and privilege to receive you, My Liege,' Morville said. 'To Henry Plantagenet, King of England, Duke of Normandy, Duke of Aquitaine, and Lord of Ireland.' He raised his goblet in toast as he spoke and king, earl, barons, knights and men-at-arms drank as one. Silence fell over the gathering.

Henry glanced around, seeming to enjoy the discomfort of the assembled men, and prolonged it further by taking a large gulp of Morville's finest Rhenish and helping himself to a large portion of venison. The others took this as their cue to help themselves, although Tracy and Brett in particular found their appetites diminished by the atmosphere in the hall.

It was a great honour to host the King, but they could not help but reflect that Henry had arrived incognito. He wanted no one but his most trusted men to know of his presence in Cnaresburg. That did not bode well.

Henry looked around the almost silent hall, then said, 'It may be advisable to dismiss your men-at-arms before I continue.' He stared at Morville and FitzUrse, and all four knights gestured to their sergeants. A noisy five minutes later, the only men present were the nobles and their king, although Mauclerk hovered behind his lord.

Chapter 30

'What news have you of Canterbury?' Henry began.

'None, My Liege,' Morville said. 'We receive little word of events here in Cnaresburg. What has occurred?'

'Miracles. At the Archbishop's tomb. Healings. There is talk of canonisation.'

'A saint? They talk about making a traitor a saint?' FitzUrse exclaimed.

'So it seems,' said Hamelin Plantagenet. 'It appears that however high Becket was raised in life, you have raised him further in death.'

Morville opened his mouth to speak, then closed it when no words came forth.

'But he was a low-born clerk,' FitzUrse said. 'He stood against the Young King!'

'And was murdered before his altar!' Henry roared. 'Within the sanctuary of his cathedral!' He slammed his fist on the table then stood, heaved up the platter of venison, and hurled it to the floor. 'You have made a holy martyr of him!' He swept his arm across the tabletop, scattering trenchers, meat, goblets and full flagons of wine. Tracy squeaked in protest, then fell silent at his king's glance.

Henry leaned both fists on the table and bowed his head, then pulled himself up to his full height, and turned to glare at his knights.

'I gave Mandeville and Humez a simple task. Arrest Becket and bring him to me. I would have dealt with him. Instead you interfered. I have lost my battle with the Church over the Constitution of Clarendon and will not now be able to hold the English clergy accountable. I was even under threat of excommunication and eternal damnation! Four more troublesome knights I have never had!' He slammed his fist on the tabletop once more. 'I would have you all executed did I not think that would ensure my excommunication!'

'Excommunication? My Liege, that would be unconscionable,' Morville ventured.

'Apparently not. The four of you were excommunicated on Holy Thursday.'

Silence.

'But that was three months ago. We have been damned for three months?' Tracy whined.

Henry laughed. 'Three months is nothing, William. Your soul is damned for all time!'

Tracy refilled his goblet and downed the wine in one. Morville, FitzUrse and Brett followed suit.

'What did you expect?' Henry shouted. 'You had all pledged fealty to Becket, then you murdered him. In his cathedral! Did you not expect the Pope to react?'

'Just as he pledged fealty to King Louis of France, then took his wife Eleanor and half of his lands,' FitzUrse whispered to Morville.

'What was that, Reginald?' Henry asked.

'Naught, My Liege,' FitzUrse simpered. 'I am gladdened our excommunication did not extend to you.'

'Well it might have.' Henry frowned. 'Well it might have.'

The men paused, each taking another drink and contemplating: *What to say next?*

The King broke the silence. 'I suggest you each commit yourselves to earn back Rome's favour.'

'How do we do that?' Tracy asked. Henry frowned. 'My Liege,' he added.

'I would not know, although I suggest building and improving churches would make a noble beginning. Rome responds to the chink of coin,' Henry said, sitting down. 'The louder the better.'

Tracy nodded and emptied his goblet once more. He appeared close to tears.

'There is also talk of the four of you serving the Poor Fellow-Soldiers of Christ and of the Temple of Solomon in the Holy Land for a period exceeding ten years.'

'The Knights Templar, My Liege?' FitzUrse and Morville protested together.

'Fear not. It is unlikely to come to that. But the whole of Christendom wishes to see you punished. They need to believe you are contrite. Although if you do not build enough churches—' Percy and Courcy grunted and suppressed laughter '—you may have to serve if you wish to save your souls,' Henry warned.

'You need to tell Pope Alexander what he wants to hear and keep the Saxons quiet,' Hamlin Plantagenet added. 'Do not embarrass our king any further.'

The knights nodded, chastened.

'You must present yourself to Pope Alexander at your earliest convenience. Do what you can to repair your reputation – and mine – before then,' Henry ordered.

'Yes, Sire,' the knights said.

'We shall take our leave,' Henry said, rising once more, and the knights escorted him and his party to the bailey and their horses.

'There will be a joust of peace at Riche Mont Castle in a sennight,' Henry said, mounting. 'Do not attend. Do your penance before you show your faces again.' He dug his spurs into his mount's flanks.

Morville held his breath, but his men were paying attention and the gates to Cnaresburg Castle opened as King Henry reached them.

Chapter 31

25th July 2015

Helen took a deep breath and opened the door to Spellbound.

'Oh hello,' Donna said from behind the counter. 'How are you?'

'Hi, I'm fine, thanks,' Helen said, then hesitated. 'Well, not really, to be honest.'

'What's wrong?'

'You remember that spirit board I bought from you?'

'You'd better come through,' Donna said, and pulled back the curtain from the alcove behind the counter where she did her tarot readings. 'Take a seat,' she said, and took the far chair for herself. 'Tell me.'

'You know feva is coming up?'

Donna nodded.

'I'm with the Castle Players and we're putting on a play about Morville and the other knights who murdered Thomas Becket then hid out at the castle here.'

'I see,' Donna said, drawing the words out.

'The guys were having trouble connecting with their characters and I thought the spirit board would be a fun and different way to embrace them.'

'I told you when you came in, the Ouija is not "fun" – it's serious and you need to treat it with respect.'

'I know, I know, and I did – I followed all your instructions.'

'And the others, did they take it as seriously?'

Helen said nothing.

'Let me get this straight – are you telling me you used the spirit board to contact a medieval king, four of his knights and the priest they murdered, as – what – a theatre game?'

'Exercise rather than game,' Helen said. 'And it worked, the improvement is amazing! I thought at first that they'd let go, relaxed and embraced the characters, but now . . . now I think it's something more.'

'Why?'

Helen took a deep breath. 'Everyone's . . . changed.'

'Changed – how?'

'Well, Dan and Sarah have split after ten years and two kids – and it's nasty. He's become aggressive and belligerent, which he never was before, and Sarah . . . Well, Sarah's lost her mind. She's taken up with one of the other guys – someone she's always been friendly with. I reckon he's fancied her for years, but she never felt the same.'

'Are you sure?'

'Yes. I can't count the number of times we've talked about him and she's always thought he was sweet, but boring. He never did anything for her, and now she's besotted.'

'Is there any correlation between that and their characters?' Donna asked.

Helen thought for a minute. 'I guess so. It's hard to know for sure, the historical record's sketchy at best, but Sarah plays Richard le Brett, who served William de Tracy, who Mike plays. They were the meekest of the four knights, so it stands to reason they were close.'

'And the husband?'

'Dan plays Reginald FitzUrse – a brash, vulgar bully. Which is what he's turned into.'

Donna nodded but remained silent awhile before asking, 'And what of the others?'

'Well, Paul and Charlie – they play King Henry and Becket –

they're acting oddly too. They were always good friends with plenty of banter, but lately it's more – they're so competitive it's unreal, and Paul's getting to be a right pain, throwing his weight around and taking everything over.'

'Just like a medieval king,' Donna said.

'Exactly. Alec and Ed – to be honest, I'm not sure, with the drama of the others, I've not really noticed.'

'So what in particular prompted you to come and see me?' Donna asked.

'Last night there was an argument over money – Charlie's the treasurer – and Paul practically accused him of stealing. It echoed an argument between Henry and Becket and it was just one coincidence too many. I think they're possessed.'

'Possessed is a strong word and unlikely, but it *is* possible that spirits have attached themselves to your friends.'

'What does that mean?'

'They're here, feeding off the energy of their "hosts" and influencing their behaviour.'

'But how can that be? Henry was a Norman king, he didn't speak English, and the English language that Becket knew bears little resemblance to the one we speak today. How can they be influencing the speech and actions of men they can't communicate with?'

'But Charlie and Paul speak English. Language is a function of our brains not our spirits. The guys are just tools for the spirits to use. One more question, did you close the spirit board?'

Helen looked down at her hands.

'You didn't, did you?'

'We couldn't. Something happened—' she paused and Donna waited for her to continue. 'It was weird, it was like an explosion of – nothing. But we were sent flying. I fell off the stage and broke my wrist,' Helen pushed back her sleeve to show her tatty pot, 'everybody else landed on their arses, and the spirit board just vanished.'

Donna drew in a sharp breath. 'And you haven't found it?'

'No. To be honest, we didn't look very hard – we were all freaked out. I was hurt, and I don't think any of us actually wanted to see it again.'

'You have to find it. That's what is connecting the spirits to your friends.'

'So if we find it, then what, destroy it?'

'Yes, burn it and cleanse the place where you held the séance – was it at the theatre?'

Helen nodded.

'We'll also cleanse each individual and hopefully it's not too late.'

'What do you mean, too late?'

'It sounds like the connection is strong. It's unusual for spirits to exert so much control unless the person is in trance. Judging by their history, the spirits have unfinished, extremely emotional, business to put right. When was the murder?'

'1170.'

Donna released a breath and seemed to shrink into herself. 'So that's what, eight hundred years?'

'Nearly eight hundred and fifty.'

'That's a long time for unresolved issues to brew, even in the spirit world.'

Helen didn't know how to reply to that, so said nothing. Then, 'How much will it cost?'

Donna glared at her, then her expression softened. 'Don't worry about that at the moment – the main thing is to stop the spirits replaying their past or exacting vengeance, and make sure everybody is safe.'

'Safe? You think we're in danger?' Helen asked, horrified.

'They've already hurt you and broken relationships,' Donna said. 'God knows what else they're capable of – it sounds like they're gathering strength every day.'

Chapter 32

'Hi Donna, thank you so much for doing this,' Helen said as she let the Wiccan into the theatre.

'No problem. How long have we got before the others get here?'

'About an hour.'

'That should be fine, but let's get started. Where did you hold the séance?'

'On the stage.'

'Of course you did.'

'What do you mean?' Helen asked.

'Oh I'm sorry, there's no need to be defensive.' Donna laid a hand on Helen's arm. 'It's just that the spirits were given centre stage – it will have given them extra energy. You know how you feel during a show – that high?'

'Yes.'

'All that energy over countless shows – by everyone who's ever performed there – leaves an energetic signature behind. Over the years that would have built up, and when the spirits were invited to join you, it would have given them a sizeable boost. That's probably why they were able to get rid of the spirit board and attach themselves so firmly. Did you look for the board?'

'Yes. Yes I did, but I couldn't find it.'

'Maybe one of your friends took it and put it "somewhere safe".'

'But why would they do that?'

'They didn't – the spirit they're hosting did.'

'Oh.'

'Not being able to deal with the board makes this much harder. Keep an eye out – especially when visiting your friends. See if you can find it.'

'Okay. Will this work without it?'

'That depends on how strong they are and how badly they want to see this through.' Donna frowned, then brightened and smiled to reassure Helen. 'Only way to find out is to try. Let's get started. The stage first.'

Helen took a deep breath, then followed Donna through the auditorium and up to the stage where she deposited the large bag she was carrying.

'What's all that for?' Helen asked as Donna pulled out bundles of herbs, a lighter, dish, coloured candles, a box, and a cup ornate enough to be labelled a chalice.

'I'll cast a circle first,' Donna said, picking up the ornate box. She opened the lid and showed Helen the contents. 'Salt,' she said. 'It will start to purify the place.' She walked around the stage area in as large a circle as she could fit, sprinkling the salt as she went.

'That covers the main area of the stage,' she said. 'Whatever you do, don't step out of the circle. I'll cleanse this area first, then go around each part of the theatre, then outside.'

'Okay,' Helen said, feeling like an extra from *Supernatural.*

Donna bent, picked up a compass, and checked that she was in the exact centre. 'Will you put the green candle there, it represents earth,' she said, pointing. 'Left a bit, perfect,' she added as Helen did as she was told. 'Now the yellow candle in the east for air. Then a red candle for fire to the south and blue for water in the west. Then come to the middle and stay still.'

Donna picked up one of the bundles of herbs and the lighter.

'Sage,' she said by way of explanation. She walked to the green candle and lit it, muttering under her breath, then round to light the others, ending up back at the green candle. She held the bundle of sage to the flame until it caught, then blew on it until it smoked copiously with no flame.

'With earth I cleanse this place of fear, pain and anger. Henry Plantagenet, Thomas Becket, Hugh de Morville, Reginald FitzUrse, William de Tracy, Richard le Brett, thank you for your time here, please leave now. We send you home and invite light, love and peace to dwell in this place,' she intoned, walking around the circle anticlockwise, then she came back to the centre, placed the herbs in the dish, and picked up another bundle.

'Cedar,' Helen said, recognising the smell when Donna lit it.

Donna said nothing but repeated her chant as she walked around the circle waving the smudge stick.

'Sweetgrass,' Donna said as she lit the next bundle, this time walking clockwise.

Helen looked nervously at the amount of smoke and made a mental note to check the smoke alarms. *Surely at least one of them should have gone off by now.*

Donna blew out the candles, and Helen strained to hear what she was muttering – it appeared to be a number of thank yous.

'Now for the rest of the theatre,' Donna said with a smile, picked up the still-smoking bundle of sage and wafted the smoke into every corner and along every boundary of the stage, auditorium and the areas backstage.

'Are we done?' Helen asked, checking her watch – the others would be here soon expecting a rehearsal not a Wiccan ritual.

'Not quite, I'll go outside and do the same all around the building – everything I can get to, anyway,' she said, referencing its semi-detached nature. 'Then I'll need to do each member of the cast.'

'What? They'll never agree to that, not the way they are now,' Helen said.

'Then find a way to persuade them – and do it on the stage – that has received the most intense cleanse and the spirits' hold on them should be weakened.' Donna recognised the distress in Helen's face and hugged her, careful to keep the burning herbs well away from their bodies. 'Don't worry, I'll help you fix this.'

Helen nodded and sniffed, surprised to find herself emotional. 'Thank you,' she whispered.

'Have a drink of water and just sit quietly and gather your thoughts,' Donna said. 'I'll be back soon.'

Helen jerked in surprise. The smoke alarms were finally doing their job and an ear-splitting howl transformed what had been a tranquil moment into a nightmare – at least until she realised what the noise was.

'What the bloody hell's going on here?' Paul demanded. 'Dan, shut that thing off will you?'

Dan waved his script under the sensor to clear the smoke, and the alarm silenced. Until another emitted a high shriek. One by one they were silenced. One by one they screamed.

Finally, a quiet that lasted. Until Paul broke it.

'Well, Helen? Are you going to tell us what in the name of God you've been doing?'

'Actually, that was me,' Donna said from behind him.

He spun around and stared at her – eyes insolently examining her from her short blonde hair, down her long pink dress, to her pointed black patent boots, then back up. 'And who the hell are you?'

'Hi, I'm Donna,' she said brightly, holding out her hand for a shake. 'From the Wiccan shop.'

Paul kept his hands by his sides, then slowly turned back to Helen and arched an eyebrow in question.

'Come and sit down, everyone. We need to talk,' Helen said, indicating the circle of chairs she'd arranged at the centre of the stage.

'Come on, mate,' Charlie said, tugging at Paul's arm. 'Let's see what she's got on her mind.'

'I don't have time for this,' Paul said.

'Of course you do. Stop moaning and sit – whoa.' Charlie dropped Paul's arm and stepped back as Paul's hand bundled into a fist.

'Sorry, mate,' Paul said after a moment and relaxing his hand. 'Don't know what's got into me lately.'

'That's kind of what I need to talk to you about,' Helen said and led the way to the circle of chairs.

Chapter 33

'This is Donna,' Helen said loudly enough that everyone could hear her, 'from Spellbound.'

'A witch?' Charlie said, his voice full of disgust.

'Wiccan,' Donna corrected. 'Very different to what the Church portrays as a witch.'

Charlie muttered something under his breath that sounded remarkably like, 'Heathen'. Donna glanced at Helen but did nothing else to acknowledge the comment.

'A few weeks ago, you experimented with the spirit world,' Donna said.

'Load of nonsense,' Dan scoffed.

'I don't think so,' Helen said. 'Since then, you've all been . . . different.'

'Different how?' Ed asked.

'Well, for one thing you've become your characters on stage—'

'That's what we're supposed to do,' Paul said. 'We're actors!'

'—and offstage,' Helen continued as if he hadn't spoken.

'How do you mean?' Sarah asked, and Helen narrowed her eyes. *Surely Sarah out of everyone realises what's going on?*

'Well, as you said yourself, Sarah, the friendship between Paul and Charlie has changed – you're far more competitive with each other than before.'

Paul and Charlie looked at each other and shrugged.

'And you yourself, Sarah – it's no secret that Mike has fancied you for months . . .'

'Hey,' Mike said, but Helen ignored him as well as Dan's cursing.

'But you've never entertained him as anything but a friend before – now you've moved out and are seeing him. It's just not you!'

'I bloody knew it, you cheating bitch!'

'Is there any point to this?' Paul interrupted, holding a hand up at Dan to quieten him.

'Yes Paul, there is a point, you're not in control.'

'So you're saying this . . . this *mess* is down to, what, ghosts?' Dan asked.

Helen's heart sank at the tone of hope in his voice. Whatever the reason, what had been done had been done and there was no going back from it. 'Yes, that's exactly what I'm saying.'

'So all this, the breakup of my marriage, my kids' heartache, mine, it's all because you brought that, that, *thing* here and made us use it?'

Helen had no answer.

'No,' Donna said. 'Many people use spirit boards every day with no problem. Unfortunately, the spirits you contacted are angry, powerful and have no doubt waited centuries for a chance to come back and put right what was done in their lifetimes.'

'So just bad luck, huh?'

'I'm afraid so.'

'What can we do about it?' Charlie asked, his voice hesitant as if he had to force the words out.

'We've cleansed the theatre, and now, with your permission, I'll cleanse you. But to be honest, it may not be enough. We need to find the spirit board too – do any of you know what happened to it?'

'It just . . . disappeared,' Ed said and Donna stared at him.

'Do you know where it disappeared to?'

'No, of course I don't. I'd have said.'

'Okay, shall we start with you for the cleansing?'

'What? I-I don't know about that, what does it involve?'

'It's nothing to be worried about – I'll just cleanse your aura with sage and ask any spirits to leave.'

'Sounds like pagan devilry to me,' Charlie said.

'Pagan yes. Devilry no. Everything I do comes from a place of light and love,' Donna said.

Charlie's thoughts were clear enough on his face that he didn't need to voice them. Donna glanced at him nervously then turned her attention back to Ed.

'Okay, I want you to uncross your legs and arms, close your eyes and relax. Just concentrate on your breathing and let any thoughts drift away.'

Ed looked relaxed enough and Donna took a smudge stick from her bag, then lit it. She wafted it around Ed, surrounding him in smoke, then placed the sage in a dish and stood behind him, hands on his shoulders and face upturned. 'I call on my angel guardians and spirit guides to join with Ed and cleanse him of the spirit of . . .' Donna opened her eyes and looked at Helen in question.

'Hugh de Morville.'

Donna repeated the name, then repeated the mantra twice more as she waved her hands rapidly upwards from Ed's feet to the crown of his head, finally clapping her hands together above his head.

She placed her palms back on Ed's shoulders and asked him how he felt.

'Okay, I guess,' he said slowly, blinking as he refocused on the group. 'Yeah, okay.' He smiled up at Donna, who moved to Sarah, carried out the same ritual then went on to Mike.

'You're not touching me, witch,' Dan said as Donna finished Mike, stood in front of him and picked up the sage.

'I won't harm you,' Donna reassured.

'I don't care, you're not casting your spells over me!' He hit out, catching Donna's hands and she dropped the smoking bundle of herbs.

'Dan!' Sarah shouted. 'Stop it, she's only trying to help.'

'You don't get to tell me what to do any more, whore,' Dan sneered. 'What you think and want is nothing to me, do you understand?' He jumped to his feet and Sarah recoiled in her chair.

'Fucking heathen bullshit,' Dan said and kicked the bundle of herbs off the stage.

'Dan!' Helen cried and ran offstage to retrieve the bundle. 'You'll set the place on fire.'

'Oh stop bleating, woman! It's always melodrama with you. I'm going to the pub, anyone want to join me or would you rather chant spells and set fire to yourselves?'

'Reginald's right,' Paul said. 'Hold on, I'm coming too.'

'And me,' Charlie said and they both followed Dan out of the theatre.

'Did Paul just call Dan Reginald?' Sarah asked.

Helen nodded, her face ashen.

'Things have gone too far,' Donna said. 'This is more than I can deal with.'

'So what do we do?' Helen asked.

'I'll make some calls,' Donna said. 'But to be honest, I think the only people who can stop this are Dan, Paul and Charlie.'

The others stared at her, then at the exit door.

'Fat chance of that happening any time soon,' Mike said, then pulled his chair closer to Sarah's and put his arm around her. 'You okay, love?'

'You have to find that spirit board, Helen,' Donna said. 'It's probably your only chance.'

Chapter 34

'Dan! Dan, wait up! Where are you going?' Paul shouted.

Dan turned. 'Harrogate. Had enough of Knaresborough for one night. I can't stand seeing those two huddled together. I want some real pubs – and some real women – preferably ones I don't know.'

'Amen to that,' Charlie cried. 'Wait up, we're coming with you. Next bus in what, five or ten minutes?'

'There it is,' Paul shouted. 'Come on!'

They ran in front of the bus, preventing it from leaving the stop outside Sainsbury's, and giving the driver no choice but to wait and let them board – though he clearly wished to avoid it.

'Onward, Coachman, á Harrogate,' Paul cried and the three of them creased up in laughter. The young woman sitting near them got up and made her way to the front of the bus where she felt safer, which only amused the three actors further.

Half an hour later, a relieved bus driver pulled into Harrogate bus station and opened the doors. He'd expected more trouble than raised voices and raucous laughter, but was glad to wash his hands of the three unruly men nonetheless.

'Where to?' Charlie asked.

'I fancy somewhere grand but cheap,' Paul said.

'Wetherspoons then,' Dan said. Situated in the historic Royal Baths, once a place visitors flocked to in their thousands to sample the Harrogate spa waters, the pub had kept the soaring decorated ceilings yet boasted the same prices as any other Wetherspoons in the country.

'Lead on, my good man,' Paul said, sweeping his arm expansively.

'So what the hell was all that crap about?' Dan said once they all had full glasses in front of them.

'Devil worship,' Charlie said.

'Women's troubles,' Paul said and raised his glass. The other two spluttered, clinked, then drank.

'Another round, boys?' Paul said, eyebrows raised. They had all drained their glasses.

'Keep 'em coming, Sire,' Charlie said, and they burst into laughter once again.

'So what's going on with you and Sarah, Dan?' Paul asked.

Dan scowled and thumped his glass on the table, sloshing red wine on to the polished wood.

'What's there to say? She's shacking up with that bastard, Mike.'

'What? She's moved in with him?'

'Well, she reckons she's staying with Helen until I move out, but she'll be with him.'

'And she's making you move out?' Charlie asked.

'Yeah. Then no doubt she'll move lover boy in.'

'And you've agreed to this?' Paul asked, incredulous.

'No choice.'

'Why?'

Dan shrugged. 'If I don't she'll go to the police, tell them I hit her or something.'

'And did you?' Charlie asked.

Dan looked uncomfortable then, 'Fuck, yeah I did.' He drained his glass. 'We were arguing about Mike, then she ignored me to answer his call.'

'Sounds like she deserved it,' Paul said.

'Damn right she did, embarrassing me like that, and with a mate. I should do it again!'

'She's making a fool of you, Dan.'

Charlie noticed the looks of disdain from the women on the next table and felt uncomfortable for a moment, although he wasn't quite sure why. He ignored the feeling. 'All right, darling?' he said and the women pointedly turned their backs. He laughed and went to the bar.

'Bloody hell, he's pulled,' Charlie told Paul, half a dozen glasses of wine later. Paul turned in his seat to see Dan at the bar talking to a group of women, two bottles of red wine on the bar beside him.

'It doesn't look like he's bringing them over,' Paul said.

'What? The wine or the girls?'

'Neither!' Paul stood up too quickly and knocked his chair over. He left it where it was and lurched to the bar, Charlie in his wake, bowing and making apologies for his friend, though not caring if he received glares or smiles in response.

Paul approached behind two of the women and cupped their hips as he pushed his head between them to greet Dan. 'Aren't you going to introduce us?' he said, oblivious of the women recoiling from him – one of them straight into Charlie's arms.

'Forgive my manners,' Dan said. 'These are my good friends Henry and Thomas.' He raised his glass to Paul with a wink and a smirk. 'And I'm Reginald.'

'You mean you've been hogging these lovely ladies and haven't even introduced yourself, uh, Reg?' Paul asked, laughing. 'Hey, where do you think you're going?' he added as the woman lucky enough to avoid Charlie's clutches almost succeeded in freeing herself from Paul – who just gripped tighter. Hard enough for her to cry out and push him away.

'All right, that's enough, leave the ladies alone.' A short but burly man dressed in a black suit grabbed hold of Paul's shoulder.

'And who might you be?' Paul said, his voice full of disdain.

'I'm the bloke who's kicking you out. You can go quietly, but if not my friends and I will help you on your way.' He jerked his head towards the door but did not take his eyes off the drunken men.

Paul pushed closer to him. 'You do not lay a hand on me or my friends, do you have any idea who I am?'

'I don't give a shit who you are, you're not welcome here.'

'You insolent . . .'

The doorman caught Paul's swinging fist easily and used his momentum to spin Paul around, twist his arm behind his back, and propel him towards the doors.

'Hey, you can't do that,' Charlie shouted, moving to come to his friend's aid. 'He's King Henry!'

'Yeah, he's King Henry and I'm William the Conqueror,' the doorman muttered, all patience evaporated – if he'd had any in the first place.

'He is.' Dan descended into giggles as two more security staff grabbed him and Charlie and marched them all out of the pub, the crowd of patrons parting before them.

'You're not welcome back,' the first doorman said. 'So don't even try it.'

'Why, you cretin,' Paul said, lunging for the man and catching him on the jaw with his fist. The doorman quickly wrestled the 'king' to the ground, kneeling on him to keep him subdued while his two colleagues dealt with Charlie and Dan's drunken and ineffectual attempts to free their friend. Soon all three were on the ground amidst a growing circle of concerned onlookers.

Within minutes a police van arrived and the doormen let the three friends up. They immediately spun again, but the men were expecting a clumsy attack and stepped back to avoid it. Each actor was grabbed from behind by police officers, then thrown against the side of the van, where more officers fastened handcuffs on their wrists.

'I am arresting you for being drunk and disorderly,' one of the officers – a sergeant – said. 'And if you don't calm down, I'll add assault to that. What are your names?'

He received only verbal abuse in return and indicated that the officers should put them into the back of the van.

When the cage door was shut and locked behind them, the sergeant tried again. 'What are your names? It'll be worse for you if you don't answer.'

'Reginald FitzUrse,' Dan said and cackled with laughter. 'And this is Thomas Becket and Henry Plantagenet.'

'I see,' the sergeant said with a sigh. 'At least that's more original than Mickey Mouse.' He shut the van door and thumped on it to indicate that the driver could go, then turned to ensure the pub security staff were okay and ask what the hell was going on.

Chapter 35

July 1171

The knights and their men-at-arms gathered in the outer bailey; the marshal and grooms in a flurry of activity to ensure the horses were tacked and ready to ride. One of Tracy's men lost his battle with the frayed nerves of his mount and it bolted; scattering men, weapons and horses until it was brought up short by the curtain wall.

Morville and FitzUrse glanced at each other in despair at the chaos.

'Just as well no one attacked or laid siege,' said FitzUrse. 'All that training and it's a shambles.'

Morville shrugged. 'No one knows what to expect, and you all have a long journey ahead – especially Tracy. Plus the men don't know what to think – I'd be surprised if you didn't lose a few on the road.'

'When I find out who told them of the Pope's sanction, I'll strangle him with my bare hands,' FitzUrse said.

'You would never keep that news quiet,' Morville said. 'The whole kingdom is aware.'

'Yes, well, this shall not be a comfortable ride.'

'Think of poor Tracy. When you and Brett arrive in Somerset he still has almost a sennight's ride to his estates in Cornwall.'

'It seems an awful lot of trouble to go to – all to build a few damnable churches.'

'The King wishes it. We need his favour and that of the nobles. I just hope it shall be enough to pacify Pope Alexander.'

'You know Tracy is talking about building three,' FitzUrse said.

Morville shook his head. 'Damned fool, can't do anything in moderation.'

FitzUrse shrugged. 'He's keen, too keen at times, but you know he'll always do his best for you.'

Morville stayed silent as Tracy and Brett approached.

'Are you ready, Reginald?' Tracy asked. FitzUrse gave a curt nod. 'Then we bid you farewell, Hugh.'

'Godspeed and safe journey,' Morville said. 'I shall see you in a month or two.'

'Yes, and all of us considerably poorer,' FitzUrse said.

'It is a small price to pay to regain the favour of all of Christendom,' Tracy said. No one could gainsay Tracy's piety, although FitzUrse scowled. Morville rested his hand on his fellow knight's arm to forestall any rebuke.

'Godspeed,' he said again. 'Build your steeples tall and your naves wide. Let these churches be a beacon to sinners and saints alike.'

'Amen,' Tracy said, crossing himself. The three knights turned to go, FitzUrse at the rear shaking his head. Morville suppressed a smile. Despite The Bear's outward show of scorn, he had not overly protested at riding to Barham Court to raise a church dedicated to Thomas Becket as his declaration of repentance. He was as shaken by the news that Becket was to be canonised as he was by his own censure.

Once his guests and their retainers had cleared Cnaresburg, Morville set out on his own mission of penance.

'What made you settle on Hampsthwaite?' William de Stoteville asked.

'It is a new parish and growing, yet has not a stone church,' Morville replied, 'and is close enough to also serve the new hamlet of Clint.'

'Would not a church serve you better in Cnaresburg itself?'

'Cnaresburg has the church of St Mary Magdalene and Nostell Priory. It needs not another place of worship and would likely be seen as a bribe by the populace.'

'You may be right,' Stoteville said, surprised that Morville had thought this through.

'The population of Hampsthwaite has grown in recent years and a stone church would fulfil a true need. A much better penance do you not think?'

'Yes, I do indeed.'

'Although I have charged Robertson of Cnaresburg as master stone mason and given him full authority over his team of masons.'

'And he is happy to carry out the work?'

'There are few commissions of this size to be had. He is very happy indeed.'

'And so shall many families in Cnaresburg be happy,' Stoteville said with a wry smile at Morville's cunning. 'Which will go a great way to restoring your good name.'

'Let us pray it is so,' Morville said. 'If I can turn the hearts of Yorkshiremen, turning the heart of an Italian pope shall be a simple task in comparison.'

Stoteville laughed as Morville kicked his horse on into the ford through the River Nydde at Hampsthwaite, and followed him into the shallow water.

A few yards further and Morville pulled up his mount to the right, where the current chapel was situated. 'We shall replace this shack. Those woods shall supply the timber for the fitments, it is near the heart of the village and by the crossroads, so also easy for the folk of Clint to attend,' he said, glancing around at the abundant green fields and woodland, and the small wooden structure already standing.

'But it is not on a rise,' Stoteville objected.

'No,' Morville said. 'I do not want to put my church above the village.'

'Becket's Church,' Stoteville could not help but correct.

'Indeed,' Morville said.

'The ideal spot. Ah, here is Robertson now.'

'That went exceedingly well,' Stoteville said on their return journey to Cnaresburg at dusk.

'Yes, Robertson is very pleased with the opportunity – especially as I did not object to the number of masons he wishes to employ,' Morville said.

'If it brings harmony back to Cnaresburg Castle, it is a low price to pay,' Stoteville said.

'Yes, my thoughts exactly. Although I am concerned about how many carpenters Foster will foist on me when he hears of it.'

'Your pockets will be much lightened,' Stoteville observed with a smile.

Morville sighed. 'What price Heaven, William? For let us face it, that is what I am buying.'

Stoteville could find no answer and they rode in silence.

'What's that?' Morville exclaimed as he topped the rise of the hill leading to Bond End.

Stoteville joined him. 'God's bones – fire!'

Both knights kicked their spurs into their horses' flanks and galloped into Cnaresburg.

The marketplace, surrounded by flimsy thatched timber buildings, was well ablaze and both men stared in shock.

'Go to the castle!' Morville shouted. 'Raise the garrison, maybe we can save the rest of the town.'

'But what if it's a trap?'

'It's no trap, William, hurry!'

'But Percy or even Courcy could have instigated this to weaken your defence of the castle.'

'They would be more direct, William. Tarry no longer, to the castle with you!'

Morville jumped off his horse, giving the rump of Stoteville's a hearty smack as he did so.

'Hurry, before I have to rebuild the whole town,' Morville shouted, then joined the line of men and women passing buckets.

Stoteville galloped down Butter Lane and Castle Gate to the gatehouse, his horse spooking at flares of ashes and airborne embers.

As he led the garrison back out, he remembered Morville joining the line of peasants and shook his head. He had underestimated his brother-in-law.

Approaching the marketplace at the head of a column of men-at-arms, Stoteville spotted Morville, black with soot and dirt, grasping the arm of an equally encrusted man, and he grinned. Morville had done much to repair his reputation and standing this day.

A thought flitted across his mind. He dismissed it but it would not leave him be. *Had that been Morville's plan?*

Chapter 36

26th July 2015

Helen looked at her watch. 'Well, we can't wait any longer, let's get started.'

'How can we rehearse Becket's exile scene without Becket or Henry?' Ed asked.

'Not very well, clearly,' Helen snapped, then she sighed and ran a hand through her hair. 'Sorry, Ed. Everything just seems to be falling apart.'

'It's the ghosts.' Mike chuckled.

'Don't laugh, love, it probably is,' Sarah said, her hand on Mike's knee.

Helen sighed again. Nothing had changed much since Donna's cleansing — not enough, anyway. 'We'll talk through all the practical stuff, use this time to get everything sorted.'

'I don't see why they can't be here,' Alec grumbled. 'We're all giving up our time and Paul and Charlie have the leads.'

'I'll ring again, see if I can find out what's going on,' Ed said and left the theatre to find a signal.

'I think we need to expand plan B,' Helen said. 'Just in case things don't get any better.'

'They can hardly get worse,' Alec said.

'What do you have in mind?' Sarah asked.

'Understudies,' Helen said.

'You have got to be joking, Paul and Charlie have the leads!'

Mike echoed Alec's earlier words. 'Most of the play is the two of them! It's not the same as understudying Dan.'

'What do you suggest?' Helen retorted. 'Cancel the show?'

'No way, being part of feva is massive for us, I'm not walking away from it,' Alec said.

'Are you willing to understudy then?' Helen asked.

Alec sighed and looked around at the others. 'I guess so,' he said. 'I know Henry's part best, I'll learn Paul's lines. But that means somebody else will have to understudy Dan.'

Helen breathed a sigh of relief. 'Thanks, Alec. Mike, how about you? It's you or Ed for Becket.'

'What about me or you?' Sarah asked.

'I'll take one of the knights' roles if need be,' Helen said.

'John or Kate might take one on,' Sarah said.

'Yes, fantastic.'

'Why can't I play Becket?' Sarah asked again.

Helen stared at her. 'I think we can get away with women playing the minor roles, but having a woman playing a medieval archbishop won't go down well.'

Sarah pouted and sat back in her chair, arms crossed, but didn't argue.

'I'll do it if Ed refuses,' Mike said grudgingly. 'But with work and all I'm not going to have much time.'

'Thanks Mike, I appreciate that. We'll ask Ed when he comes back in, but to be honest we've got some serious work to do to pull this together for opening night.'

'Plan A or plan B?' Sarah asked, still petulant.

Helen was saved from having to answer by Ed running back into the auditorium. 'They were all arrested last night!'

'What?' the others shouted, all but Sarah who frowned and shook her head.

'Tell us, Ed,' Helen said, fighting the urge to weep as she saw everything she'd worked so hard for fall into ruin.

He gave them the story, then added, 'They've been charged with drunk and disorderly, but wouldn't accept a caution, the stubborn idiots. So it will go to court. They've been knocked around quite a bit apparently – Paul's spitting feathers, talking about suing Wetherspoons and the police.'

'Bloody typical,' Alec muttered.

'How badly hurt are they?' Helen asked.

'Not sure to be honest, Paul was too busy ranting about the police.'

'They'll be fine then,' Sarah said. 'And Dan?'

Ed shrugged. 'They'll be here soon. You can ask him yourself.'

'I need a coffee,' Sarah said and stood. 'Anyone else?'

'I need a bloody bottle of wine,' said Helen and everyone laughed. 'I guess coffee will do for now though.'

Sarah led the way back into the theatre. 'The convicts are coming,' she said amid peals of laughter. Her husband, Paul and Charlie followed, carrying the coffees and scowling.

'Give it a rest, Sarah,' Helen said, noting the expression on Dan's face in particular. 'How are you doing, guys?'

'Battered, bruised, knackered,' Paul said. 'How do you think?'

An awkward silence fell on the group.

'At least you're here,' Sarah said. 'Why don't you sit down and have your coffee?'

Dan glared at her, but the others took seats at the front by the stage.

'So what happens now?' Helen asked.

Charlie shrugged. 'We have a court hearing in a couple of weeks.'

'What, like a trial?' Sarah asked.

'No, just a hearing. I think we just say not guilty, then it will go to trial a few months later.'

'A few months? So after feva?' Helen said.

'Yes, after feva, Helen,' Paul said, sarcastically. 'The show won't be affected.'

'Sorry, Paul. If there's anything we can do to help, you only have to ask. And honestly, the show's already been affected,' Helen said.

'We were just talking about plan Bs,' Alec said. 'I'm to be your understudy, Paul, you know, just in case anything else goes wrong.'

Paul said nothing, his face unreadable.

'And who's to be my understudy?' Charlie asked.

'I'm not sure, it's between Ed and Mike,' Helen said. 'And I'm sorry guys – it is only plan B. So much has already gone wrong, I'm just trying to be prepared.'

Nobody said anything until Ed broke the silence. 'I'm happy to do it – not that I expect I'll be needed,' he said, looking at Charlie, who nodded.

'So who's my understudy?' Dan asked.

'Helen,' Sarah said, not quite hiding the glee in her voice at the dismay on Dan's face. There was a reason Helen stayed offstage.

Silence again.

'Shall we get on then?' Paul asked. 'Can't sit around here gossiping all day.'

The resultant laughter broke the tension and Helen gave him a grateful smile before briefing them.

'Becket's exile,' she began, but Paul interrupted.

'The year's 1164 at Northampton Castle. Becket's gone too far and thinks Henry is a tyrant. Henry is determined to bring him to heel. Becket's conduct has crossed into treason with a lot of insults and bickering. Nothing is achieved. Becket's been embezzling – which reminds me, Charlie, have you done those accounts yet?'

'Sod off, Paul, I've been a bit preoccupied of late, I'll bring them next time.'

Paul nodded then turned back to Helen. 'Where was I? Oh yes, embezzlement. Attack and counter-attack. Vicious war of words, Becket grovelling.'

'Hardly grovelling,' Charlie said. 'Making sound legal argument and proposing excellent compromises.'

Paul waved his friend's words away. 'Then Becket – guilty coward that he is – flees to France.'

'It's a little more complicated than that—'

'Okay, okay,' Helen interrupted. 'You know the scene, do you want to take the stage and run through it?'

'See – you're worrying about nothing,' Sarah said, leaning toward Helen.

'I hope you're right.'

Chapter 37

'No, guys, that's not high enough,' Helen said. 'I want Henry overlooking the murder, saying the words that drove the knights to Canterbury. He needs to be higher, overlooking the entire scene, almost godlike. I want to draw the parallels between the two great influences over everybody in England – the Church and the Crown – and the conflict between them.'

'But you said the platform just needed to be raised a bit,' Alec protested.

'It doesn't sound like that was what she said. Just admit it, you cocked up!' Ed said. 'All that work for nothing.'

'Don't go putting all the blame on me,' Alec said. 'You were there too.'

'No I wasn't, I was off getting the swords and other stuff.'

Helen held up a hand to forestall further protests. 'I don't care whose fault it is, we don't have time for blame. Opening night is in one week – we need a higher platform. Henry needs to be above the heads of everyone else – the position he believed he held.'

'But that's a massive job,' Alec protested. 'Can't we just make do?'

'Make do? Are you kidding me?' Ed shouted. 'All the work we've put in and you want to make do on the final scene – the scene it's all been building up to?'

Alec shrank back from the venom in Ed's voice. 'Sorry, it's just . . . I don't know how we're going to do it in time, along with everything else.'

Before Ed could tell Alec exactly what he wanted him to do, all three were distracted by more acrimonious voices backstage.

'Stay here and work it out,' Helen said and dashed off towards the sounds of the screams and shouts, leaving Ed and Alec bickering despite the commotion.

'What the hell is going on?' Helen demanded, rushing to Sarah who sat on the floor in a huddle together with John and Kate. She looked to Dan for an explanation, but he stood silent, fists clenched and face red.

'Mum asked Dad for a divorce,' Kate said solemnly. 'Dad didn't take it very well.'

Speechless, Helen looked from Sarah to Dan and back again. *They've done this now? And in front of their kids? What the hell is wrong with everyone?*

Helen's blood ran cold as the thought registered, then took control of herself. 'Dan, go and help Ed and Alec, they have a problem with the set for the final scene and need an extra pair of hands.'

Dan didn't move.

'Go, now Dan. I'll sort everything out, just go and help the guys.'

Dan finally looked at her, nodded, and left, all without saying a word.

'What's going on?' Mike rushed over to Sarah. 'Love, what happened?'

In answer, Sarah's sobbing increased. Mike took her face in her hands and drew in a breath through clenched teeth. 'He hit you again, didn't he? The bastard! I'll sort him out!'

'You'll do nothing of the sort, Mike,' Helen said. 'Stay here and look after Sarah. John, Kate, can I have a word with you?'

The teenagers looked to their mother – a silent question if she was okay – then followed Helen. Kate was shaking, John trembled with rage.

'Come and sit down,' Helen said, and led them out to the auditorium, choosing seats out of earshot of everybody else. The argument between Ed and Alec was still going strong on stage – she wouldn't be overheard.

'I know everything's a mess, but don't blame your parents,' Helen began.

'Are you *serious*?' John asked. 'Dad *hit* Mum – in front of us, we *saw* him.'

'And it's not the first time,' Kate said. 'Mum keeps getting bruises and lies about them.'

Helen took a deep breath, shocked that things were far worse than she'd realised. 'Your dad isn't well,' she said, then stopped at the looks of scorn from John and Kate.

'It's difficult to explain,' she tried again. 'But this is my fault and I'll fix it.'

'How is it *your* fault?' John asked.

'When we started rehearsing, I tried something a bit different to help everyone get into character.'

'Oh, the spirit board,' Kate said. 'Yeah, Mum told me about that.'

'You're not serious? Why are you messing about with that stuff?' John asked.

Helen sighed. 'I know, it was stupid, but – as with most bad ideas – it seemed like a good one at the time.'

'Are you trying to tell us that Mum and Dad are what – possessed?' John asked incredulously.

'Not possessed exactly,' Helen tried to explain. 'But I think the spirits of their characters have . . . attached themselves to everybody.'

'Attached? What does that mean?' Kate asked.

'I'm not sure I understand it properly myself, but somebody is trying to help me sort it out.'

'So you're saying that Dad is really FitzUrse, and Mum is Richard le Brett?' John asked.

'Well, in a way, yes. For the moment.'

'Does that mean Mike's gay?'

Despite herself, Helen choked a laugh and the teenagers joined in.

'I doubt it, everything is just . . . mixed up at the moment.'

'What do you want us to do?' Kate asked.

'I want you to get out of here – can you go and stay with your grandparents for a while? Your nan's in Harrogate isn't she?'

'Um, yeah, we've been staying there anyway but I'm sure she'll let us stay longer. What are we supposed to tell her? Hi Nan, Mum and Dad think they're medieval knights and we're scared to be around them?'

Helen laughed again, then realised it was inappropriate and stopped. 'Maybe not that – just say your parents need some alone time.'

John nodded. 'Okay.'

'But what about the costumes? I'm helping Mum with them and we haven't finished,' Kate said.

'Don't worry about it – I'll help your mum finish them. I just want you both out of the way and safe.' Helen reached over and gripped their arms. 'Trust me. I *will* fix this. Then your mum and dad will be back to normal.'

'Promise?' Kate said in a small voice.

Helen took a deep breath then nodded. 'Yes,' she said. *Shit, what have I just said?* she thought.

Chapter 38

August 1171

'Horsemen!' The lookout on the tower of the east gate shouted, and the cry was echoed to the inner bailey where Morville was going through his paces with sword and Mauclerk. He stepped back and removed his mail hood.

Mauclerk panted with exhaustion for a few seconds and followed suit, but his lord was already running to the tower, despite his mail tunic and recent exertions, to see for himself.

Up in the battlements he peered into the morning sun. 'Can you make out who it is?' he asked his sergeant-at-arms.

'Not yet, My Lord. Maybe when they approach Brig-Gate.'

Morville pointed; children were running towards the castle, their faces and voices excited and hearty. 'They are friends not foes. Open the gates.' This last a shout, and minutes later the heavy gates were unbarred and swung open, the portcullis was raised, and the drawbridge dropped.

FitzUrse was the first through, followed by Brett and an assortment of their men-at-arms and retainers, all looking weary but relieved to have arrived. Tracy followed, escorting a cart, in which Morville was surprised to see a woman holding two newborns. He guessed this must be the wife Tracy had been bleating on about when in his cups. Finally some good news – Tracy had healthy twins.

'Reginald, William, Richard, welcome! It is good to see you

again, my friends. How was your journey?'

'Long,' FitzUrse said. 'The less said the better.' He looked behind him at the gates, still open. 'I was surprised by Cnaresburg's welcome. It appears things have changed.'

'They have. I am in favour again, at least in my own town.'

'Although not to the extent of leaving the gates open,' FitzUrse interrupted.

'No harm in a little caution. How went it with you?'

'Difficult,' FitzUrse said. 'The bastard masons tried to charge me at least triple, the carpenters more still. I refused. Tracy fared the worst, insisted on funding three churches, the fool. They've left him near penniless, but at least the weeping and wailing when he's in his cups is reduced to bearable proportions, although he cares about naught but his wife and the babes now.'

Morville laughed, put an arm round each of FitzUrse and Brett's shoulders, and addressed Tracy as he guided them to the keep. 'Come, your old bedchambers are ready for you. I'll have baths prepared, then rest awhile and I'll have Jack organise a feast for dinner. Plumton and I took a venison a sennight since. It's well hung and will serve.'

'Jack is back?'

'Yes, as are they all, down to the serving girls. Sheepish and eager to please, just how I like them.'

The men guffawed and climbed the narrow stone stairs to their respective bedchambers, Tracy solicitously aiding his wife.

'Ah, I am ready for this,' FitzUrse said, striding to the lord's table. 'Those bastards at Teston virtually besieged me in the manor house, it has been some time since I sat at table like this.'

'You should have paid them what they wanted, Reginald,' Tracy said. 'Ease tempers rather than inflame them.'

'Ah, but then I would not have been able to make a loan to you, William.'

Tracy coloured and glanced at Pomperi, who diplomatically turned to Helwise with a compliment about the stones-and-roses decoration on the walls of the great hall.

'It is but small and temporary,' Tracy said.

Morville interrupted before tensions rose higher between the two knights. 'And what of you, Richard, how did you fare?'

The young man shook his head and grabbed his goblet to drink.

'Sir Simon barred the gate to him,' FitzUrse answered in Brett's stead. 'Refused to acknowledge him. The boy lived as an outlaw in Sampford Brett, despite the place carrying his name. Sir Simon only admitted him once the first stones of the new church had been laid.'

Lost for words, Morville drained his own goblet and called for more of the fine Rhenish wine.

FitzUrse grabbed the serving girl as soon as she deposited full flagons on the table, and pulled her on to his lap. 'This is better, Hugh, too much hard muscle on a man-at-arms to be serving table.'

Morville's men, seated below the knights in the body of the great hall, roared with laughter, every one of them relieved to be sitting to dine rather than cooking and serving.

'Beyond Teston,' Morville said with a glance of frustration at FitzUrse, 'our favour appears to be growing once more.'

Tracy and Brett nodded. FitzUrse ignored the jibe and wrenched a huge mouthful of venison from the joint before him.

'Yes, England is becoming friendly again,' Tracy said with a fond look at his wife. A smile flitted across Pomperi's face and Morville wondered at the strain apparent on her countenance. He glanced at his own wife and for the first time recognised the marks of a similar strain on her features.

'And not before time,' FitzUrse said, the words fighting their way out around the half-chewed meat in his mouth.

Morville forgot his inspection of the women and reconnected with his train of thought. 'I think it's time to call on that favour and grow it further,' he said.

'What do you have in mind, Hugh?' Tracy asked.

A slow smile spread on Morville's face and he paused before answering, judging his timing well. 'A tournament,' he said. 'Tourney for the nobles and a fair for everyone else.'

'God's wounds, Hugh, a tourney! Just what I need. But a real one, a proper joust of war and a mêlée. If we do this we do it well.'

Morville grinned. 'Just as I was thinking, Reginald. A real spectacle, something for all to enjoy.'

Brett clapped his hands together with a grin.

'Is that wise?' Tracy asked. 'We have risen in favour due to repentance, would not holding a tournament risk losing it again, especially from the Church?'

'Nonsense, William. Why, even the parish priest attended at Harewood. The Church's position on tournaments is posturing, naught else.'

'Maybe so, but remember what else happened at Harewood,' Tracy persisted.

'How could I forget?' FitzUrse said, and pointed a half-gnawed bone at Tracy. 'One tourney unmade us, another will remake us. Nothing gladdens a noble's heart more surely than a tournament done correctly, with proper ransoms and every opportunity to shine. Now, to business. Where would be the best place to host the mêlée, Hugh?'

As the men plotted, Helwise and Pomperi held each other's eyes for a moment, the despair in each clear enough to require no accompanying words.

Chapter 39

September 1171

'Fortune has smiled on us,' Brett said. 'It is a good sign the sun has joined us.'

'Yes, and soon so will the nobility of England,' Tracy said.

'You have decided this tournament is a good thing then, have you, William?'

'Yes.' Tracy couldn't quite meet FitzUrse's eyes. 'It looks as if the townsfolk are enjoying the fair already.'

The others squinted into the morning sun. The field ahead was filled with striped tents of every colour. Blue and yellow, red and green, orange and white. Morville counted the peaks of the apexed canvas 'roofs'. 'Over a score. Good, and plenty of people too.'

'Any knights?' Tracy asked.

'Not that I can see, but they will still be on the road, I don't expect the nobles to arrive until afternoon.'

The knights entered the fair grounds and dismounted, leaving Mauclerk to see to the securing and well-being of their palfreys.

The noise and activity of the fair gave them a moment's pause; each recalling the occasions they had been shunned, by commoner and noble alike. The sight of so many people gathered together at their behest was welcome indeed.

The local tradesmen had erected tents – butcher, baker, candlestick maker amongst them – and minstrels and stilt walkers added to the chaotic atmosphere, each desperate to bring custom to their benefactor's tent of wares or goods. The more their benefactors sold this day, the more they would themselves earn.

The knights walked past a small enclosure where a group of children were pitting their cocks against each other – the youngsters almost as raucous as the birds.

'A quarter-penny on that one.' Morville indicated a bedraggled-looking bird missing a sizeable quantity of feathers.

'Hugh, are you crazed? It's barely standing,' FitzUrse exclaimed.

'Are you taking my wager?' Morville asked.

'Assuredly. Let me see.' FitzUrse scanned the birds, ignoring the expectant faces of their young owners. 'That's the one.' He pointed to the largest, preening its feathers.

Morville accepted the wager and both men gave quarter-pennies to Tracy to hold.

As the children chased down their cocks to place them in the fighting circle, Morville remarked, 'It looks like this is the first fight for yours, Reginald.'

'Yours looks like it's lost every fight it's engaged in.'

'To me, he looks like he's come out of a good scrap still standing.'

'We shall see,' FitzUrse stated. 'I stand by my choice.'

'And I mine,' Morville said.

Both cocks were released and FitzUrse's brute charged Morville's scraggy favourite. It uttered a loud squawk, jumped in the air, clipped wings flapping, and met Brute's challenge with extended talons. Another squawk and beating of feathers made it clear Scraggled's tactics were effective. FitzUrse said nothing but looked a little worried. Scraggled did not back off but continued his offensive, jutting his sharp beak into the side of his opponent, yanking out feathers with every peck.

'Come on, Brute, fight back damn you!' FitzUrse roared above the noise of the children's insulting encouragements to both birds.

Scraggled was remorseless. A veteran of many cockfights, as Morville had rightly assessed, he knew well the only way to avoid pain and injury was to inflict pain and injury. And he did so, remorselessly and unflinchingly. Within minutes, Brute lay near dead and bleeding in the fighting circle, the victor strutting and preening even fewer feathers.

'Well done, Hugh.' FitzUrse made an exaggerated bow to the victor, and Tracy passed the two quarter-pennies to Morville, who in turn flicked them both to the boy who had gathered his prize cock in his arms.

'Well done, boy, you breed them well.'

'Thank you, My Lord,' the boy said, his embarrassment at being addressed by the controversial Lord of the Manor of Cnaresburg evident in his red cheeks.

Morville glanced at the boy staring at his unmoving prize cock. 'Here, lad,' he said, and flicked another quarter-penny in his direction. 'Let this be a lesson to you, the quality of the warrior is not evident in his armour, but in his strength of heart and his will to win. Look for those qualities in the next cock you bring to fight.'

'Thank you, My Lord,' the boy squeaked, scrabbling in the dirt for his piece of coin. 'I surely will.'

'Percy,' Brett said, interrupting them. The other three knights looked up to see William de Percy striding towards them.

'He doesn't look happy,' Tracy said. 'And why is he on his own?'

Morville and FitzUrse glanced at each other, both aware that this did not augur good tidings.

'Greetings, My Lord Percy,' Morville said. The formality of his welcome was not lost on anybody present and even the cocks seem to hush their squawking.

'Greetings,' Percy replied, but gave no smile. 'What were you thinking, Hugh?'

'In what regard, William?' Morville replied, incensed at being called into question within the hearing of the children and citizens of Cnaresburg.

'A joust of war? Really? You are in need of King Henry's favour, so why flout his ban?'

'Ban?' Morville asked, his heart sinking.

'Yes, ban. Jousts of war are banned in England, and have been for some time.'

'But . . . Harewood? And Riche Mont?'

'Special dispensation from the King and jousts of peace for the practice at the quintain and ring,' Percy said.

'I, uh, we were not aware,' Morville said.

'I told you it was a bad idea,' Tracy said, and FitzUrse elbowed him so hard he staggered to keep his feet.

'You know you are out of favour, why did you not ascertain the current state of affairs before sending your invitations?'

'Why did you not advise us when you received yours?' FitzUrse said. 'It was a fortnight since, yet you only advise us now.'

Percy turned and stared at The Bear. 'I have only last night returned from Normandy. Enjoy your fair, My Lords, but there shall be no tournament. When Henry hears of this, and no doubt he has by now, you will be even further in disgrace. Good day to you, and good fortune, you are all in dire need of it.' Percy turned and strode away. The four knights stood, rooted to the spot in shock, unable to voice a sound.

'I told you it was a bad idea,' Tracy said again. 'I told you. We were making good progress, and now look, we've defied the King. Ruined, we are all ruined.'

'Hush, William!' FitzUrse shouted, his face red and fists

clenched. 'Stop your whining, or by God I will stop it for you!'

Tracy stepped back, partly in surprise at FitzUrse's reaction, partly in fear.

'Calm yourself, Reginald,' Morville said. 'This is a time for clear heads.'

'Everything we've done, everything we've endured, and now we've gone against the express wishes of the King,' FitzUrse shouted. 'He shall not forgive this easily.'

'He will understand,' Brett said. 'We were ignorant of his ban, he will understand that.'

'Understand? What the devil makes you think King Henry is understanding? Do you know nothing? He is a man who does not need to understand, he is *King!* Events are as he decrees, no matter the truth of them. He sent us to silence Becket, which we did, and look how we've been treated since. Has he taken responsibility for his part? No. It has fallen on us, his loyal servants.'

'If his character is as you say, then why has he left us here to live? Surely it would serve him better to have us dead!' Tracy said.

'Care what you say, William. He may well yet decide on that course of action.'

'But, but, we were acting at his behest!' Tracy protested.

'What does that matter? A year ago Becket was a troublemaker, an impious archbishop intent on sedition. Now he is a martyr and will no doubt be canonised. We killed him in his cathedral, before his altar. When his body was prepared they found his hair shirt, so he is no longer impious. Now he is a devout man whom we killed in God's sanctuary. When we dealt with him he was hated. Now he is loved. Where we were loved, now we are hated.' FitzUrse stopped, overcome by his passion and words.

Tracy gaped at him. Morville and Brett looked on, both silenced by FitzUrse's analysis of their situation.

'What are we going to do?' Brett whispered, his querulous tone betraying his youth. Morville felt sorry for him: he had not yet seen his twenties, but had dealt the killing blow and Morville could see no future worth the pain of living ahead of him.

Silence, then: 'We go to the Pope. We throw ourselves on his mercy and take what punishment he decrees,' Tracy said.

'By God, no,' FitzUrse shouted. 'It is Henry we need to appease, not the Church.'

'We are excommunicated. Our souls are damned for eternity,' Tracy said. 'By your very admission, King Henry does not need to understand, he will do what is most propitious for himself. If we are pardoned by Pope Alexander, we will be pardoned by King Henry.'

'Don't be so sure,' Morville said. 'From what I have learned of our king these past months, I feel he would consider himself injured if we put the approval of the Pope over his own.'

'Yes, you speak well, Hugh,' FitzUrse said. 'I am in agreement.'

'I am not.' Tracy drew himself up to his full height. 'And I will no longer follow your lead, Reginald. You led us here. I will leave for Rome to prostrate myself before His Holiness Pope Alexander. I will prepare Pomperi and the babes, escort them to Bovey Tracy, then take my leave of England. Will any of you accompany me?'

Morville said nothing, Brett would not meet Tracy's eyes. FitzUrse was the only one to speak, once again holding the fate of his companions in his hairy fist. 'You are on your own, William. We shall take all necessary steps to regain King Henry's favour before we attend to Pope Alexander.'

Tracy drew in a sharp breath. 'Very well. I bid you good fortune and hope our paths shall once again cross.' He walked away, slowly but deliberately, having finally chosen his own path, at the age of thirty seven.

Chapter 40

30th July 2015

Paul stood stage left, spotlighted and dressed in purple tunic, hose and crown, a short cloak slung about his shoulders. Helen smiled – that faux fur had been a wonderful find in the charity shop, and Paul looked every inch the medieval king, strutting in his leather boots.

She looked up as Donna sat in the seat next to her. 'Sorry I'm late.'

'Not at all. Thanks for coming. We're just building up to the final scene.'

'Ah, England's fine shores,' King Henry proclaimed. ' 'Tis good to be treading her fertile soil once more. Come, Henry,' he called offstage to his son. 'This will all be yours one day, 'tis time to claim your rights as my heir.'

The light on Paul doused, and a new spotlight shone on Charlie, sitting stage right, dressed in a brown monk's habit and with a table of papers before him.

'Ah, Henry, my old friend, you test me so,' Becket said, reading a scroll. 'You insist on insulting my Church and my Pope – not to mention my good self. What to do with you? How to bring you to heel?'

The lights switched once more, illuminating Henry standing, legs apart and arms akimbo. 'This is *my* kingdom. *I* rule here and no other. My son shall be crowned as my heir and I shall brook no argument. Close the ports!' He swept his arms wide. 'Becket can stay in France, cowering from my wrath. He shall not oppose me in this too.'

He turned and began to pace the distance of the lighted area. 'With the ports closed, neither he nor any messenger can defy me. Not even communiqués from the Pope can be brought. I shall have no interference from the Church in this matter.'

Back to Becket, now joined by an uncomfortable-looking Sarah dressed in a nun's habit.

'Mary de Blois, my dear Princess, you are my only hope.'

'Archbishop, I am pleased to serve you, Your Grace.'

'I have a task for you. A task only you can succeed in, and you shall have your retribution against Henry for the unholy marriage he forced upon you.'

'I need no retribution, Your Grace. I only wish to serve our Lord in the company of my sisters.'

'Indeed,' Becket said. 'Both myself and Pope Alexander are most grateful that you have chosen to leave the convent to assist us.'

The lights switched once more. Paul had now been joined by Ed playing the role of young Henry – the King's eldest son.

'Prepare yourself, boy, this is a great honour.'

'Yes, My Liege,' Ed said, playing a bewildered boy terrified of a tyrannical father.

Henry adjusted the ermine cloak his son wore, then looked up in fury as Sarah walked into the light.

'What is the meaning of this?' he roared.

'I am a royal princess, Sire, daughter of King Stephen and your cousin. Your closure of the ports could not stop me attending the coronation of young Henry.'

'I see,' Henry said, his eyes narrowed in suspicion. 'Have you brought Rome's blessing?'

'Indeed I have not, Sire. I hold papal decrees for Archbishop l'Évêque, Bishop Foliot and Bishop Salisbury,' Sarah said, producing three scrolls bearing the intersecting circles of the seal of Rome. 'They are forbidden to continue with this coronation in the absence of the Archbishop of Canterbury.'

'Ah, so Thomas still thinks he has power over me, does he?' Henry said.

'Indeed not, Sire, only over the bishops who are subordinate to him,' Sarah – as Mary de Blois – said.

'Hah,' Henry shouted. 'Becket holds no power in a land in which he is too cowardly to set foot. The bishops are subordinate to *me!*' He grabbed the scrolls and ripped them, throwing the pieces back into the nun's face. 'The coronation shall proceed. My son shall be proclaimed the Young King this day.'

The stage plunged into darkness and Helen stood, applauded carefully as the lights came back on – grateful her pot had finally come off – and shouted, 'Well done, guys. Sarah and Ed, you could both be a little more relaxed on the night, but well done!'

Helen sat back down and turned to Donna. 'What do you think?'

Donna sighed. 'It's not good news, I'm afraid. Both the main guys had spirit with them – I've never seen spirits so close to a living man before. They didn't just stand behind or to the side, they walked in.'

'Walked in?'

'Yes. Almost blended with the men. Have you ever seen a trance medium work?'

Helen shook her head.

'It's quite remarkable to witness. The spirit of the medium withdraws and gives permission for another spirit to enter – at least temporarily.'

'That sounds . . . frightening,' Helen said.

'No – it's done with permission and great respect, and the trust is never betrayed. The disembodied spirit needs the full approval of the medium. But here . . .' she paused. 'This is something else. I've never seen anything like it. The auras of both the main men—'

'Paul and Charlie,' Helen said.

Donna nodded. 'Their auras changed as soon as they started speaking. Even their appearance changed, did you notice?'

Helen stared at her hands and did not speak.

'When they finished . . .' Helen looked up at Donna, waiting for her to gather her thoughts. 'The spirits withdrew,' Donna continued, 'but not completely, they're still attached by their auras.'

'Is that bad?' Helen asked.

'It isn't good,' Donna said. 'Especially as I don't think the guys are even aware of it. I think this is without their permission and they're being violated.'

'So what do we do?'

'We hold another séance and ask the spirits to leave.'

'And will they?'

'That depends on how strongly and faithfully Paul and Charlie tell them to go.'

'Faithfully?'

'If it's a deep and genuine wish to be left alone.'

'And we need their cooperation and belief?'

'Yes.'

'They don't believe.'

'That they want the spirits to withdraw?'

'That the spirits exist in the first place.'

'Then we really do have a problem,' Donna said.

Chapter 41

'Okay, let's pick up from where we left off yesterday,' Helen said. 'We have a few days left, let's make them count. Places everyone.'

Paul and Charlie walked on to stage, Charlie taking Becket's place to the right, Paul to the left. The rest of the cast settled into their seats to watch, Dan sitting as far away as possible from his wife and Mike.

Helen turned to the sound and lighting booth to give Alec a thumbs up. 'From the top.'

Charlie's spotlight focused its glare on to Thomas Becket. He sat at a table, scroll in hand, and paused as he read, then looked up to the audience, stood, and brandished the parchment.

'By God, that man shall drive me to apoplexy! His son is crowned – *crowned* – and by a hand other than mine! The lion of justice? No – a rat of betrayal! He shall be the death of me, by God, I swear it.'

Becket approached the front of the stage and lowered his voice. 'But I shall not submit to his tyranny. Yes, *tyranny*! Once my good friend, he has become a caricature of himself – of a king. I shall bring him back to actuality – bring him back to himself, the good man he once was. I shall save him if it is the last thing I do.'

Becket returned to his chair, picked up a quill from the table and began writing on parchment. The spotlight dimmed and Henry's blazed into life.

'Damn that man!' Henry shouted, both fists clutching sheaves of parchment. 'Will he never do my bidding? Look at these, *look* at them!' He thrust the parchments towards the auditorium. 'Papal mandates, letters of interdict from Becket and Pope Alexander! They're threatening excommunication. Imagine, *me*, Henry, King of England, excommunicated! It's unthinkable!' He threw the parchment into the air as he stamped his foot, grabbed fistfuls of his hair and cried out as if in pain as he doubled over.

Straightening, he calmed and his hands dropped to his sides. 'I have no choice. I must extend peace to Becket and bid him return to England. That should take care of these.' He kicked at the scattered parchment. 'At least in England he shall once again be within my reach.' He smiled in cunning.

Becket's spotlight came on and the men met centre stage and embraced as the lights dimmed to nothing.

'That was great, guys, well done,' Helen called to the stage, standing and clapping. The other Castle Players did the same.

Helen turned to give Alec a clap too, the complicated lighting sequence having been executed perfectly, then spotted another audience member at the back of the theatre. 'Donna! What are you doing here?' Helen said as Donna stood and moved to join her.

'What's she doing here, *again*?' Dan called and made his way to join the rest of the crew. 'Come to do an exorcism?'

Donna shook her head. 'No, no exorcism, you're not possessed by demons, but are being attacked by spirits. That's very different.'

'So why are you here?' Helen asked.

Donna gave her a strange look. 'You invited me, don't you remember?'

Helen looked puzzled and glanced at Sarah, who shrugged.

'After I called Richard Armitage and told him what was going on.'

'You did *what*?' Sarah said.

'Don't worry, he didn't believe me. Sarah, what have you done to your face?'

'Ask my husband,' she snapped.

Donna looked around at everyone, eyes settling on Dan, who looked furious. 'Can I have a word in private?' she asked Helen.

'Uh, yeah, I suppose so.' Helen looked to the others and they all drifted towards the stage and Paul and Charlie.

'What's going on?' Donna asked Helen. 'Has Dan been hitting Sarah?'

'Only a couple of times, but they're staying well away from each other now. Well, at least when they're not on stage.'

'Has she been to the police?'

'The police?' Helen looked blank. 'No.'

'Why not? She's a victim of domestic abuse.'

'I didn't really think about it like that, they'll sort it out between themselves.'

Donna stared at her in a moment. 'Oh my God, you've got one too.'

'What are you talking about? I'm fine.'

Donna lowered her eyes and looked up at Helen through her lashes. 'No, you're not. You have a man standing in your aura – too close. He's in mail so is another knight. Hang on, I'm trying to get his name. Brought, rock, something like that.'

'You mean Broc? Ranulf de Broc.'

'Yes, that's it. Who was he?'

'The Lord of Saltwood. He hosted the knights and rode to Canterbury with them, then smoothed the waters with Henry.'

'So he was the man behind the scenes? The director?'

'I suppose so,' Helen said.

'As are you.'

Helen said nothing.

'We have to hold another séance, ask the spirits to leave.'

'No.'

'Why not?'

'We open on Saturday. You saw the guys, they're good. Better than good, they're great! It could be Becket and Henry up there.'

'It *is* Becket and Henry up there! Don't you understand? We have to make the spirits leave, they're too strong, and they're still increasing their hold on their hosts!'

'Not until after the show.'

'That may be too late! Look at what's happening to you all – Dan and Sarah, Mike, you're always in the pub, and I heard your two leading men were arrested a couple of weeks ago. Your lives are already being affected, and they're getting stronger. Things will only get worse. You *have* to cancel the show!'

'No. We're not cancelling.'

'But Helen, don't you see? The spirits have such a strong hold I'm afraid they'll only leave when they right the wrongs that were done to them in life.'

'We're not cancelling the show.'

'But anything could happen. It's too dangerous to go ahead!'

'You heard. We're not cancelling the show.'

Donna looked up to see that the rest of the Castle Players had rejoined them and stood as a pack in the aisle. She turned to Helen again, but realised by the set of her jaw and folded arms that the woman wasn't listening.

'Oh God,' Donna said. 'Oh my God. It's already too late.' She hurried out of the theatre.

Chapter 42

October 1171

'How do you consider Tracy fares?' Brett asked.

Morville shrugged and FitzUrse said, 'Probably hasn't reached Rome yet.'

'What will happen to him?'

'Pope Alexander will no doubt hand him over to the Dominicans,' FitzUrse said.

'No! They would torture him, even burn him!'

'We don't know what else the Pope would order, unless it be serving at the pleasure of the Knights Templar. Percy said that Henry and Rome are on better terms these days, so I doubt he shall be given to the Dominicans. The Pope will not burn Tracy, that would necessitate taking strong action against King Henry too. He will no doubt be ordered to the Holy Land as the King suggested.'

'You think so?' Brett asked, his youth evident in his shaking voice.

Morville held up a hand to forestall FitzUrse's probable brutal reply. The boy needed encouragement, not fear. 'It is sure to be so, Richard. Do not fret, William will live, and no doubt welcome his penance, his conscience was deeply troubling to him. This is the right course of action for him.'

Brett nodded. 'Then why did we not travel with him?'

'Bah! Prostrate myself before the Church, throw myself on

179

Pope Alexander's mercy? I'm not minded for that course of action. Let us regain King Henry's favour, then he will help us with Rome,' FitzUrse said.

Brett nodded again.

'Begging your pardon, My Lord,' Mauclerk interrupted them, speaking from the door to the great hall. 'Sir William de Percy has arrived.'

'Percy? Again? Well, show him in, Hugh,' Morville said, then glanced at Brett and FitzUrse. No words were said, but all thought the same: *What now?*

Percy strode into the room, wasting little time on greetings. 'I am here on the King's business,' he said, holding up a scroll bound with ribbon and Henry's distinctive double-sided seal.

He handed the scroll to Morville then helped himself to wine. He winced at the rough Spanish vintage; he much preferred the far superior Rhenish.

'We are bid come to Ireland,' Morville said. 'We must leave at once to join King Henry's expedition.'

'Is there unrest, William?' FitzUrse asked Percy. 'With Dermot dead and Strongbow's surrender, I thought all was well.' He glanced at Morville and Brett. 'After the débâcle with the tournament, I took it upon myself to employ a number of my men-at-arms as messengers.'

'Messengers or spies?' Percy asked.

FitzUrse stared at him. 'News bearers, to ensure I keep abreast of events.'

'What has happened to occasion an expedition?' Morville asked in an attempt to defuse tempers.

'Strongbow is above himself. Yes, he surrendered but with the condition that he is granted the fiefdom of Leinster.'

'That is on the east coast is it not?' Morville asked, unwilling to admit to Percy that he had no idea what trouble Strongbow – Sir Richard de Clare – had caused to necessitate a surrender.

'Yes,' Percy replied. 'Too close to England's shores for a man with such recent aspirations as King of all Ireland. Richard de Clare is far too strong in an unruly land, Henry does not trust him, despite his promise to turn over the key ports and castles to England. Henry wishes to show Clare who is king, and to leave nothing to uncertainty.'

'And he has requested our assistance?' Morville asked, pleased at the portent of this.

'Most assuredly,' Percy said to beams of relief from the three other knights. 'He has lost much this past year. The Charter of Clarendon and the reform of clerical courts – a charter you were witness to, were you not, Hugh?'

Morville gave a small nod, saying nothing, wishing people would stop reminding him. No smiles were evident now.

'Then of course the favour of Rome, which he has had need to address with the Charter of Reconciliation. A turn of events most embarrassing and expensive to him. He wishes to keep you close so you can cause him no more harm, nor gold. The restitution he is required to make to Canterbury in particular would have paupered most nobles.'

Morville, FitzUrse and Brett glanced at each other in unease.

'We did as we were ordered . . .' FitzUrse started, but Percy held up a hand to forestall him. 'That is between you and King Henry. In this instance I am a mere messenger. We ride to Harewood to join Courcy at dawn tomorrow then on to the west coast. A ship awaits us.'

Morville rose. 'We shall be ready in good time. We are King Henry's knights, it is a great honour and we shall put our all into battle for our king.'

'Á King Henry,' FitzUrse and Brett chorused.

Percy gave a wry smile, but gave no opinion. 'Very well. I shall return at dawn with my men. Good eve to you.' He drained his goblet and strode out of the hall, leaving the three knights to stare at each other, wondering what this augured for them.

Chapter 43

It had been a hard ride, conducted mainly in silence, and every man in the party – baron, knight, man-at-arms alike – was relieved to see the gleaming blue strip of sea and smell salt on the air. Every attempt at conversation on the week-long trek had failed, and all were eager to see a change in circumstance.

The men, led by Courcy and Percy, rode on to the beach and loaded themselves, their armour, weaponry and what was left of their supplies into the small boats waiting for them.

'Do you think this means we are back in favour?' Brett asked, the three knights having managed to board the same boat without Courcy, Percy or any of their men.

'Sure to be,' FitzUrse said, full of confidence as ever. 'Henry would not have asked us to join his endeavour should he not value us.'

'Unless he means to rid himself of us under the guise of war,' Morville said.

'Damn and blast, Hugh, why do you always look at things so darkly? King Henry cannot denounce us without denouncing himself, I tell you.'

Morville shrugged. 'Very well, I hope you speak true.'

'Sure to be,' FitzUrse said. Brett said naught, but did not appear encouraged.

The Spirit of Aquitaine grew closer as the sailors pulled on their oars, and with some trepidation the knights regarded the vessel to which they would be entrusting their lives over the next stage of their journey.

She was of a good size, more than fifty feet in length, and near a quarter of that in breadth. With a single mast and large sail, she had fighting platforms fore, aft and aloft. There were no cabins. This was a warship, built for everything but comfort.

Once the goods, men and horses were loaded, there was barely space for the sailors to work. Brett, never a good sailor, ensured that he had a place against the side, knowing he was likely to spend the voyage across the Irish Sea hanging over the rail, and hoping he had picked the right board. The last thing he, or any of his fellows, wanted was a youngster vomiting into the wind.

At last the anchor was hauled up, the sail loosed, immediately catching the wind, and *The Spirit of Aquitaine* started her voyage west. To glory or humiliation, no man knew, but every man aboard determined to believe in glory.

'I don't understand why King Henry is invading Ireland,' Brett said, clinging on to the side of the ship. 'What are we facing?'

FitzUrse heaved a large, dramatic sigh, as if in exasperation, but said nothing.

Morville suppressed a smile. He realised The Bear didn't fully understand either but was loath to admit it. 'All I know is what Percy told us,' he said, then started as Mauclerk joined them.

'It appears Strongbow was sent to represent King Henry's interests,' Mauclerk said. 'But then allied himself with King Dermot, insisting, or forcing, that he be made his heir. Dermot died, and sure enough, Strongbow was named. The high king, Rory O'Connor, did not accept that, but Strongbow routed him on the battlefield.'

'How do you know all this?' FitzUrse demanded, his distaste of Morville's clerk clear.

'I ask questions, My Lord. And I listen to the answers,' Mauclerk replied, staring at FitzUrse.

'Continue, Mauclerk,' Morville said, disinterested in FitzUrse's dislike of his most loyal man.

'King Henry ordered Strongbow home to England, but he did not obey, so the King placed an embargo on supplies to Ireland – including men.'

'What did Strongbow do?' Brett asked.

'Nothing,' Mauclerk said.

'And Henry will not have a baron call himself king, of any land,' Morville said. Mauclerk gave a small nod. 'And so he mobilises his knights into an army and we take Ireland.'

Mauclerk nodded again.

'Some army,' FitzUrse said, watching Percy and Courcy, 'when two of Henry's most trusted lords avoid all unnecessary time in our company.'

The four men stared at the two nobles, chilled by the fact – hitherto unremarked – that they had made a place for themselves as far away as possible in the confines of the deck of *The Spirit of Aquitaine*.

'Ugh, the wind's getting up,' Brett said, hauling himself to his feet then being violently sick over the rail. Thank goodness he'd chosen the right board, the wind blew at his back and the contents of his stomach were swept away from the ship, deck and gathered knights.

'Umm,' Morville said, the tang exacerbating his own distress as his stomach disagreed with the more urgent lurch and wallow of the ship's motion.

'Oh calm yourselves, it is a gentle breeze, is all,' FitzUrse scoffed.

Morville jumped to his feet and joined Brett over the rail to empty his stomach. He sat back down and could not resist a glance at Percy and Courcy. They appeared to have found a subject of much merriment; Morville feared he knew the cause.

The wind continued to increase as *The Spirit of Aquitaine* fought her way west. As she did so the waves deepened and the warship may well have been a cork navigating rapids. Within minutes, knights and men-at-arms alike were spewing. The horses, gathered and tethered amidships, squealed their terror, their hooves threatening to stave in the boards of the stinking deck.

One – Hugh de Morville's finest destrier – reared, snapping the rope securing him, and the men closest to those flailing hooves screamed in alarm, having no weapons to hand and no room to run.

The stallion's distress increased the fear in the rest of the herd, and soon the waist of the ship was a mass of panicking men, horseflesh and blood, as the frightened animals kicked out.

Morville, FitzUrse and Brett stared in astonishment, with no idea how to calm the beasts in such confined quarters.

'Clear the way,' a voice roared, and men-at-arms and sailors parted to let Sir William de Percy through.

He stepped forward, drew the edge of his sword against the throat of one destrier, then plunged the tip into the chest of another.

He kept going, and in seconds, every horse lay dead or dying on the deck.

'Heave them overboard,' Percy said. 'Our king needs us. Not horse nor man would delay us.'

Chapter 44

'The Emerald Isle,' FitzUrse said as they waited to disembark. 'Ha, the greenest things in sight are the pair of you!'

Morville and Brett ignored him and looked forward to setting foot on terra firma once again; whatever their reception by Henry may be.

Staring ashore, the town of Waterford was visible in the distance, but before that all traces of green had been commandeered by Henry's camp.

Hundreds of gaily coloured tents stretched for near a league in each direction, knights and men-at-arms milling between them; the one almost indistinguishable from the other in the basic living conditions. Each lord's entourage was marked by colour. Blue and yellow for Leicester, red and white for de Lacy, blue and white for Tyrell; every combination of colour was represented.

The sea of canvas was broken up by a mesmerising array of siege engines: mighty trebuchets towered over smaller catapults and ballistas, each of them capable of hurling enough rock and iron to batter down any curtain wall, not to mention more creative payloads such as beehives or hornets' nests; the bloody carcasses of soldiers felled in battle; or the worst of the lot, Greek fire. A substance brought from Hell, it would stick to any unfortunate until it burned out; not water nor sand would dowse it, the only chance a man had was for his friends to piss on him as copiously as possible. Of course, it would only help if they had also pissed on him, at least twice, before he'd been hit by the sticky flames. Morville shuddered. He had seen its effects more than once. The very sight of a siege engine had given him chills ever since.

The highest point of the camp was taken by the most magnificent marquee. Adorned in the red and gold of Plantagenet, it was a palace of canvas. King Henry's quarters, along with his household.

The three knights stole a brief glance at each other, the only betrayal of their anxieties, then followed Courcy and Percy down the gangplank and set foot on Irish soil.

The party of five, followed by a gaggle of men-at-arms and retinues, marched through the narrow alleyways formed by rows of tents towards Henry's abode.

Morville, FitzUrse and Brett kept their heads high and their feet moving, refusing to react to the stares of every man they passed.

'Assassins!' someone hissed. 'The traitorous assassins.'

Morville caught hold of FitzUrse's arm and heaved him forward. 'It is King Henry's opinion that is important, once we know how he holds us, then all else will too. Brawling on our first audience with him in four months would not endear us to him.'

FitzUrse controlled himself with clear difficulty, his face flushed and fists clenched white, then gave a curt nod and continued to move forward. He faltered for one pace on seeing Courcy smirk, then continued onward, staring at the Lord of Harewood until he turned his back and marched forward.

Morville and Brett glanced at each other in consternation. Morville had used the word audience, but in truth it felt more like they were about to attend their own trial and execution.

At long last, they reached the brow of the hill and were admitted to King Henry's presence. All five knights dropped to one knee and bowed their heads in deference to their king.

'Ah, I have been wondering when you would arrive, I bid you

welcome,' Henry said. Dressed in his habitual hunting clothes of hose and short tunic he strode over to the group of kneeling knights. The knights rose, the relief of Morville, FitzUrse and Brett almost palpable.

Henry grasped the hand of Courcy then Percy, wrapped an arm around each of their shoulders and led them to the high table, laden with meats and delicacies. 'How went the voyage? I hear the Irish Sea was rough today.'

'We fared well, Sire,' Courcy said.

'Some better than others,' Percy smirked.

Morville glanced at FitzUrse and Brett to see a look of consternation on their faces, no doubt mirrored on his own. Their king had ignored them.

'What think you of my siege engines? An impressive sight, no?'

'Indeed, Sire,' Courcy said. 'Strongbow and O'Connor will be in no doubt of your intentions.'

'Ha! Strongbow has already capitulated, he is due soon to pledge fealty. That upstart shall never call himself King of Ireland.'

'Indeed not, Sire. He has shamed himself and his house by his actions here.'

'Verily,' Henry said. 'Far too many do the same.' He glanced at Morville and the others. 'Now, be seated and feast while I deal with these three reprobates.'

He turned back to the three knights, each of whom now dreaded his attention.

'So, you saw fit to ignore my instructions. Only Tracy had the good sense to depart for Rome?'

'We fully intend to join him, Sire,' FitzUrse interjected.

'Once you learn of his punishment and not before, I suspect?'

'No, Sire. We had heard of the difficulties Strongbow has been causing you . . .'

'Strongbow? Show some respect. He is Sir Richard de Clare,

ensure you address him as such in future.'

'I humbly beg your pardon, Sire,' FitzUrse said, falling back to one knee.

Henry stared at him and made no indication that he should rise. He glared at Morville and Brett, who both hastily joined FitzUrse in his gesture of humility.

'What a pity you did not ignore my words spoken in anger in the way you ignored my clear direction to present yourselves to Rome.'

'Sire?'

Henry stamped his foot. 'Damn and blast it, you snivelling buggers, you know well to what I refer!'

The three knights bowed their heads, knowing from long experience not to respond when Henry was in the grip of one of his furies.

'Do you understand what you have done? *Do you?*' He screamed and hurled his goblet to the floor. Fine Rhenish vintage soaked into the fresh rushes.

'All is lost! My court reforms, the Constitution of Clarendon – all gone! The clergy will never be accountable to me now. Instead I am accountable to Rome! Me! King Henry of England, Duke of Normandy, Duke of Aquitaine accountable to a feeble old man in Rome.'

Henry paused for breath, his face puce. A steward handed him another goblet of Rhenish and he drank half of it in one swallow. Not one of the gathered knights, men-at-arms or servants made a sound nor dared to move for fear of attracting their king's ire.

He thrust his face into Morville's, who resisted the urge to flinch back from the hatred in his king's eyes and the stink of sour wine on his king's breath.

'Alexander banned me from entering a church. Me – banned from the heart of God! He threatened to excommunicate me – me! And Thomas . . .' He paused to catch his breath. 'Thomas, that brilliant, frustrating, true and treacherous friend, whom I raised up from naught. Thomas will be canonised. *Canonised!* The last word was screamed as the King lost all semblance of control; all memory of having already told the knights this news lost. He fell to the ground and hammered his fists and feet upon it. As he rolled in his fit and spilled Rhenish, only occasional words were audible: 'Saint', 'Devil', 'Friend', 'Martyr'.

The knights dared not so much as glance at each other, all shocked that their actions had reduced their king to such paroxysms of fury. They had observed such behaviour before – all the men in King Henry's service had witnessed such displays – but had never before brought their master this low themselves.

The sound of heralds' trumpets outside the canvas palace finally penetrated Henry's awareness and he stilled, rose, adjusted his clothing, held out a hand for more Rhenish, emptied the goblet in one, then took his seat, waved the knights aside and awaited his visitors, all composure restored.

'Sir Richard de Clare, Lord of Strigoil and Pembroke. Sir Maurice de Prendergast, Sir Richard Tuite, Sir John Baret.'

Four nobles entered as their names and titles were announced, removed helmets and mail hoods, unbuckled sword belts and handed them to waiting servants, then approached Henry and fell to one knee in obeisance.

Henry nodded, then the first man, Sir Richard de Clare – Strongbow – stepped forward, once again fell to one knee, then clasped his hands together as if in prayer and extended them. Henry placed his own hands either side of Clare's and grasped them for a moment.

A Bible was brought close as the men loosed hands, Clare placed his right hand upon it, and met his king's eyes.

'Sire, My Lord King Henry, I beg you to hear my oath. I pledge on my faith that I would for all days be faithful to you, never cause you injury, and would give my life to your service. I would observe my homage, reverence and submission to you completely, against all men in good faith and without deceit.'

'I, your Lord King, Henry of England, Duke of Normandy and Aquitaine, accept your fealty, Sir Richard de Clare, and grant upon you the fief of Leinster. May you serve me equally in peace and war, and with loyalty and honour.'

'I thank you, My Liege.'

Clare rose and backed away, allowing Prendergast then Tuite and Baret to take his place and make the same oath.

Once the rebellious barons had been accepted back into Henry's fold, FitzUrse stepped forward but was checked by Morville's hand on his arm. These proceedings had been negotiated and agreed in advance. Henry had no use for a spur-of-the-moment pledge of fealty from them, no matter how deeply meant. He would need to forgive them first. And that did not look likely.

Chapter 45

Morville, FitzUrse and Brett set up their tents on the outskirts of the main camp, ensuring their temporary homes were surrounded, and well-protected, by those of their men-at-arms.

They sat around the campfire with a plentiful supply of wineskins and Brett poked at the brace of coneys roasting above the fire; the only meat they had been able to find. The mood in the camp was so hostile they had forgone the supply tents and caught their own dinner in the surrounding woods; woods that had been hunted daily for weeks. There was no bigger beast left in them than the bobtail coneys, and their entire party had caught not nearly enough to feed the knights and men-at-arms. Thank goodness they had thought to bring a plentiful supply of wine in their haste to depart Cnaresburg.

'That was not the reception I had expected,' FitzUrse said at last. 'We did as Henry instructed, we carried out his orders and carried them out well. And look how we are vilified.'

'Hush, Reginald,' Morville said. 'You do not know who may be listening, this is no time to speak ill of the King.'

'Indeed it is not,' a new voice said, surprising the knights. Its owner stepped into the firelight.

'Mandeville!' Morville exclaimed.

Sir William de Mandeville, Earl of Essex, grinned, although there was nothing friendly in the rictus. A second and third man stepped up, all three dressed in full mail and helmets, swords at their sides. Richard de Humez and Ranulf de Broc. The two men who had originally been sent to arrest Becket and whom Morville, FitzUrse, Tracy and Brett had beaten to the prize. And Broc, the man who had encouraged and led them to Canterbury, then turned his back on them and left them to suffer the consequences. They had not heard a single word from him since they had left Saltwood Castle nearly a year ago.

FitzUrse glared at his old master, who stared back with equanimity; no emotion or expression evident on his face.

'What is this, Ranulf?' FitzUrse asked.

'What does it look like, Reginald?' Broc replied, his tone mild. 'You have shamed our king, and by doing so you have shamed all of us.'

FitzUrse worked his mouth for a few moments before he could find coherent words. 'We shamed you?' he said quietly. 'We shamed you? We *shamed* you?' His voice and temper rose with each utterance of the phrase.

'You did.'

'But, but, it was you . . .' FitzUrse stopped, speechless once more.

'I gave you every assistance and opportunity to arrest Becket. Yet you slaughtered him in his cathedral and made him saint and martyr. You betrayed your king, your earls and your fellow barons and knights when you did so.'

'But, but . . .' FitzUrse spluttered.

Broc smiled. 'You have much to learn about politics, my friend.'

'Friend? *Friend?* You have been no friend to me!'

Broc shrugged and unsheathed his sword. Morville and Brett stepped forward, having taken the opportunity of FitzUrse's 'conversation' to don mail and helmets. Brett slapped FitzUrse's helmet with slim nose guard on his brother-in-arm's head. There was no time for FitzUrse to don mail, but all three had kept their weapons close, unnerved by Henry's reception of them.

FitzUrse glanced around and realised Broc, Mandeville and Humez' men had surrounded their outlying camp. He was gratified to see their own men-at-arms had remained, and stood between the gaggle of knights and the small encircling army. Then he realised these same men had let the visitors through and his pleasure soured.

'So you intend murder?' FitzUrse asked Broc.

'No. Murder is despicable and unchivalrous,' Mandeville said in his stead.

FitzUrse's temper rose once more and both Morville and Brett stiffened, recognising they were being taunted into stupidity. 'Reginald, care,' Morville warned.

FitzUrse didn't hear him. Or, more likely, chose not to.

'This is your fault,' he said, advancing on Broc. 'This is all your fault.' In one quick movement he unsheathed his sword and struck. But Broc was fast and parried with apparent ease. Morville recognised a smile on his face and realised he had intended to taunt FitzUrse into striking the first blow, yet he also felt a respect for the man; he knew well from their many practices with swords at Cnaresburg Castle how strong FitzUrse's blows were. Even in his fury, The Bear's strength made little visible impact on his old master.

'To arms!' Morville shouted, drawing his own sword and stepping up to William de Mandeville. He held his blade defensively, determined not to fall into the same trap as FitzUrse. Unfortunately Brett did not have the same sense or experience, and he flailed his blade at Humez, who defended with ease, with plenty of breath to taunt the young knight further.

FitzUrse, meanwhile, had lost all sense, striking at Broc quickly and ferociously, delivering a devastating sequence of strikes. Broc's mail held up to the blows that he was unable to deflect. He would be badly bruised on the morrow, but as yet his skin was unbroken.

The surrounding parties of men-at-arms were in much the same mind as FitzUrse; months of uncertainty at the actions and manoeuvrings of their masters releasing in the familiar arena of battle. At last, all was simple. The masters of the opposing men meant to harm their own masters. They would fight to the death to defend their lord. They had all spent their lives in training for these moments. This was what they knew. This was what they did. They fought. Some with swords, others with axes, still more with maces. Whatever their weapon, they struck, parried, ducked and danced around their opponent, then struck again.

Morville and Mandeville, the eldest and most cognisant men on the battleground, were the only two who had not yet landed a blow. They circled, feinted and taunted, each determined to place the other in the wrong. Each determined he was in the right.

'Cease! Cease! In the name of King Henry, cease this madness!' Hamelin Plantagenet, mounted on a large destrier in full barding, cantered into the throng of warriors. Percy and Courcy, similarly mounted, accompanied him. 'How dare you disrespect my brother, the King? Cease, damn you!'

The men separated, lowering their weapons.

'What is the meaning of this?' Plantagenet addressed Mandeville.

'Settling an old score, My Lord,' he replied.

'Consider it settled,' Plantagenet said. 'Return to your quarters.'

Mandeville, Humez and their men-at-arms retreated, faces impassive.

'The King demands an audience with you, FitzUrse and Brett at dawn,' Plantagenet said to Morville. He glanced around. 'Where is Reginald?'

Morville searched the diminishing circle of men and could not see him. 'I am unsure, My Lord.'

'Find him before dawn.' Plantagenet wheeled his destrier around and moved off. 'There is to be no further discord,' he proclaimed. 'We are here to challenge the Irish rebels, not each other. In the name of the King!'

'In the name of the King!' shouted the gathered knights and men-at-arms, both those so recently fighting and those who, Morville now recognised, had gathered to witness it.

Morville met Percy's eyes for a brief moment. Neither spoke, then both Percy and Courcy turned their horses on the spot and followed the King's half-brother.

Brett stood, having been felled by Humez. 'Where *is* Reginald, Hugh?'

'I know not, Richard. Nor where Broc has disappeared to. We must find them before we face the King. I fear there will be no rest for us this night.'

'Here! My Lord, here!' The shout was taken up by more men-at-arms and both Morville and Brett turned as one in the direction of the cry, and hurried through the trees as best they could to see what had been found.

'No! Reginald!' Brett sank to his knees, shaking. 'Why? My God, why? He did not deserve this!'

Morville said nothing, but approached his comrade-in-arms, his own men retreating to give him room. He looked up.

Reginald FitzUrse swung and twisted at the end of a rope; his face purple in the predawn light. Very clearly dead.

'Cut him down,' Morville said.

As the body of his late friend thumped on to the mulch beside him, Morville bent over him. 'Pass me a torch.'

He held the flaming pitch-soaked branch over FitzUrse and the men around him gasped. Brett erupted into further moans.

FitzUrse had not only been hung, but disembowelled, snakes of his guts writhing around his body, still slithering from the impact of his fall.

Morville held the torch close to the face to make sure of the man's identity, and gasped. Clear in the light of the fire, the letters T R A I T O R had been written on Sir Reginald FitzUrse's forehead in his own blood.

Morville stared for a moment, then handed the torch back. 'Bury him,' he said, walked over to Brett, and hauled the young knight back to his feet.

'But who . . .' Brett said.

Morville did not answer. 'We must prepare for our audience with the King,' he said instead, marching the boy back in the direction of the camp.

'What do we do now?' Brett asked after Morville had sat him in front of the fire and forced a goodly amount of Rhenish down his throat.

'We have little choice, Richard. We stay and die as Reginald did. We flee and live as outlawed excommunicants in a vicious and strange land. Or we petition the King to allow us free passage to Rome and throw ourselves on the mercy of Pope Alexander.'

'But the Dominicans?'

'We pray that we are sent to serve the Knights Templar and not the Dominicans.'

They stayed silent for some minutes. Then Brett asked, 'What are our chances?'

Morville looked at him, shook his head, and emptied his wineskin.

'So,' Henry said, still in his hunting hose and tunic. 'Sir Reginald has departed us.'

'He has, Sire, in the most gruesome manner,' Morville said.

'A shame. He was abased when he fell. I would not have wished eternity in Hell for him.'

Morville and Brett said nothing.

'And Broc? What of him?' Henry asked the gathering of interested knights.

'Spent the night with his whore,' Mandeville said. 'He is not responsible for this.'

Henry laughed. 'Yes, that sounds like Broc.'

Morville gritted his teeth and clamped his fingers into Brett's arm to stay any reckless statements.

'Well, what to do with you two?' Henry mused, steepling his fingers and looking at his two most errant knights.

'Begging your pardon, Sire,' Morville ventured and took Henry's raised eyebrows as permission to continue. 'Richard and I beg leave to depart Ireland for Rome, there to throw ourselves upon Pope Alexander's mercy and subject ourselves to the penance of his choosing for our misdeeds.'

Henry nodded in thought, held out a hand into which was immediately placed a fine goblet of Rhenish. He took a long drink then relinquished the goblet and looked back at Morville and Brett and nodded. 'God have mercy on your souls.'

Chapter 46

1st August 2015

Donna glanced around as she handed in her ticket at the door, her hand trembling. She was relieved to see that no Castle Players were front of house, but was dismayed at the steady stream of cars entering the car park. There were too many. Far too many.

She ignored the door to the auditorium and hurried to the ladies, glad that she'd had the opportunity during the cleansing to explore all the theatre's nooks and crannies. She shut herself into the far cubicle, closed the toilet lid and sat down to wait.

By her watch there were ten minutes left before the curtain rose, giving Henry and Becket centre stage and a captive audience. She waited a little longer until she was sure no one else was in the ladies, then emerged from her cubicle.

In the hallway she took off one of her shoes – she'd worn stilettoes in preparation for this performance – took a tight hold of it and smashed the heel into the fire alarm.

She breathed a sigh of relief as the siren wailed – she'd half expected the spirits to put a stop to her plan and somehow take the alarm system offline. She felt a brief pang of pity for Helen and the other players, then hardened herself once again. However much work they'd put in, and however important this was to them, she *had* to put a stop to it. Nothing else had worked.

*

Half an hour later, huddled in the car park in the wash of blue flashing lights from two fire engines, Donna held her breath once more as Helen stood at the top of the steps with a firefighter at her side and called for everyone's attention.

Please cancel, please cancel, please cancel.

'Thank you everyone for staying, I'm relieved to announce it was a false alarm – a prank.' Helen stared at Donna as she said this and Donna glared back, her heart sinking. 'We can all go back in, the show will go on!'

Helen raised her hands to quell the surge of words her announcement had ignited and added, 'And in apology for the inconvenience, your interval drinks will be on the house.'

The crowd of theatregoers applauded and made their way back into the auditorium.

'Not you.' Helen stepped in front of Donna as she tried to re-enter. 'I know it was you, but you won't stop us. You're not welcome here.'

The firefighter stepped behind Donna, giving her a disgusted look and effectively trapping the Wiccan.

'Helen, please – you're putting the safety of all these people at risk. You can't *do* this!'

'These gentlemen would like you to go with them.' Helen indicated two police officers who stepped forward.

'Hoax fire alarms are serious, miss. If there'd been a real fire elsewhere, people could have died.'

'People will die if you don't stop this show!'

'That's a serious threat.'

'It's *not* a threat! I'm trying to stop something awful happening. These people are being controlled by spirits, they're not in their right minds!'

'I see. Have you taken anything tonight, miss?'

'What? What are you talking about?'

'Drugs, Donna. He's asking if you're high,' Helen said.

'No! Of course not. You have to believe me!'

'Come along, miss. We'll have a doctor check you out at the police station.'

Defeated, Donna allowed herself to be escorted away. She took one last look back at Helen, and saw the shape of a medieval knight standing behind her, almost melding with the director.

Helen gave Paul a thumbs up as he rushed to his new position on the balcony, then turned to Mike, Dan, Ed and Sarah. 'This is our best opening night ever, despite all that nonsense with Donna earlier. They're loving it!'

All four nodded with smiles and prepared themselves for their final scene.

Helen opened her mouth to give more encouragement, then closed it and turned to watch as the stage was lit once more.

Charlie was barely visible, kneeling before his table which had been transformed into an altar by cloth and cross.

Paul, standing on the new platform Ed and Alec had constructed, was six feet above the stage, shining in the full glare of the spotlight. He watched Becket pray for a moment then turned to the audience.

In the wings, Helen silently clapped her hands: his timing was perfect.

'A man who came to me with naught. A man I raised up from *naught* treats me with such contempt as *this!* And you, you do naught!

'What miserable and cowardly drones and traitors have I nourished and promoted that allow their king to be so shamed?

'Who here shall take vengeance for the wrongs that I have suffered? Which man that swore fealty to me, to redress all injury done to me, and pledged their loyalty and honour to me shall make good on their vow now?

'Are you so weakened by castles, wealth and comfort that you no longer care to fight for your king?

'Damn the lot of you for weaklings – allowing a troublesome, low-born clerk to treat their king with such *scorn*!

'I am ashamed to call you my vassals. *England* is ashamed of her lords! Who shall cut this canker from England's breast?'

A recording of loud male cheers and the thumping of booted feet on wooden floors and goblets on wooden tables reverberated throughout the theatre, and the knights rushed on to stage, passing underneath Henry and confronting Becket who rose to meet them as the spotlight on him brightened.

'What insanity is this, that you would enter Canterbury Cathedral bearing arms?'

'We are the King's men, come to take you to Henry to answer for your crimes,' FitzUrse declared.

'Crimes? Crimes? Of what crimes do you speak? I have committed no act that could be so described.'

'You excommunicated your king's bishops – a traitorous act! By so doing you have declared yourself against the Young King, the Crown of England, and King Henry himself!' FitzUrse turned and pointed at Henry.

Becket laughed, shook his head, and looked up at his king, who returned his stare as he braced himself on the railings of his balcony.

'King? You are naught but a small boy, stamping your foot in anger when he has lost the game!'

'What are you doing? You should not be talking to Paul! Get back to the others!' Helen hissed, gesticulating to get Charlie's attention. He ignored her.

'You have gone too far, my old friend,' Henry said. 'All I have done for you, and you betray me so heinously.'

'*I* betray *you*? You sent your knights to silence me!' Becket protested. 'You betray not only my own person but the Church and God Himself.' He smacked the fist of one hand into the palm of the other.

'Do not presume to chastise your king, Thomas. You shall only make matters go worse for you.'

Helen gave up her protests and watched silently, as did the two hundred people in the auditorium, all captivated by the two powerful men on stage.

'Cease this nonsense, Henry.' Becket indicated the stage with a wave of his arm. 'We have chased each other through Heaven and Hell for near a millennium, and now look,' Becket gestured to the auditorium, 'we are naught but a mummers' show, displayed for the entertainment of commoners.'

'You call *this* a mummers' show?' Henry asked, incredulous. 'What do you call the farce at your so-called shrine? Saint Thomas – that is the most heinous fallacy of all! You are a *low-born clerk!*' He slammed his fist on the rail, his face turning purple with rage. 'Look how you have been raised up both in life and in death, by *me!*' The last word was a roar.

'Raised up? Hounded and murdered!' Becket roared back. 'Murdered by my closest friend. And for what? Because I carried out the duties of the Archbishop of Canterbury. The duties *you* laid on me despite my protests!'

'You were my friend, my ally, together we could have transformed both England and the Church.'

'Your demands were unjust, Henry! You wanted power over the Church, nothing more. You wanted to use me to weaken the Church. You were not a king but a tyrant, too full of his own glory!'

'A tyrant you say?' Henry's voice was quiet, menacing, yet carried to every ear in the auditorium. 'You talk to me of tyranny? You, who refused the just demands of your king? You, who raised the Church against me? A low-born clerk challenging the rule of his king and *you* talk to *me* of tyranny?' Henry's voice rose in a crescendo. 'You, who damned my bishops? You, who would deny my son his crown? You, who incited the common folk of this good country against me?'

'The common folk of this country know what is just,' Becket answered, fumbling in the folds of his green robe. 'The common folk of this country need both King *and* Church. The common folk of this country have the sense to know that one without the other breeds only terror! *Yes*, I gave voice to the common folk of this country. *Yes*, I spoke and acted for the common folk of this country. And you – you still stand above them on a pedestal of your own making! You still send your knights to murder!' Becket indicated the four men behind him, a flash of light from the blade he had retrieved from his robe blinding Henry for a moment.

'Not this time! You shall not murder me again, tonight our story *changes*.' Becket threw the dagger, and laughed as the blade sank into Henry's chest, blood spurting from the wound and splattering his upturned face. 'Tonight I finally have my revenge!'

'Sire! King Henry!' the knights shouted as the audience gasped and Paul toppled over the railing of his balcony to thud on the boards below.

'You have murdered the King!' FitzUrse shrieked. 'Murderer! Traitor!'

Charlie staggered and looked around in shock, his eyes fixed on the body of his friend. 'Paul? What, what happened?' He screamed as FitzUrse's blade sank into his shoulder at the point where it met his neck.

'Dan, no!' he gasped as he fell to his knees, blood spurting from his wound.

The four knights stood and stared at the felled men in shock.

Tracy dropped his sword with a clatter. 'The King . . . the King is dead. We shall be blamed.'

'Silence, William,' FitzUrse shouted.

'But we will be blamed! You've done it again and led us to ruin!'

'Silence!' FitzUrse roared and swung his sword.

Mike jumped backwards, avoiding the blade. 'Dan, stop! What are you doing?'

'Charlie!' Sarah sobbed as she knelt beside her friend in a growing pool of blood, then looked up at her husband. 'You've killed him!'

Dan stared at his wife, then at his bloody sword and dropped it in shock. 'N-n-n-no. No. No.' He fell to his knees, hugged himself and swayed back and forth, still uttering the denial.

Chapter 47

8th August 2015

The remnants of The Castle Players walked away from the police station, down Castlegate towards the centre of Knaresborough a week later, after being questioned by the police yet again.

'Helen!'

They turned to see Donna running towards them.

'Are you okay?'

'Not really,' Helen said. 'They keep asking us the same questions, as if they think the answers are going to change!'

'Asking if we killed our friends,' Sarah added.

'It's been a nightmare,' Ed said.

'But they've let you go,' Donna said.

'Reluctantly,' Helen said. 'They couldn't charge us with anything. Everyone could, could s-s-see . . .'

Donna held Helen as she fought against tears. She'd already shed more in the past week than she had in the past year.

'They still think we did it, though,' Mike said. 'You could see it on their faces. I'm sure they're convinced we poisoned them or slipped them some acid or something.'

'But you didn't and there's no evidence of any drugs or poison.'

'No. They've put it down to mass hysteria,' Alec said. 'Blaming it on the pressure of putting on the play.'

'You know it wasn't that,' Donna said, and the others nodded.

'I'm sorry I didn't listen to you,' Helen said. 'Did you get into much trouble?'

'No, they let me go the next morning.'

Helen nodded. 'Have you heard about Dan?'

'No,' Donna said. 'What's happened to him?'

'He still hasn't spoken,' Sarah said. 'Other than repeating "No".'

'It's a catatonic state, apparently, probably to do with post-traumatic stress or something,' Mike added.

'Oh my goodness, tell me he isn't still in police custody,' Donna said.

'No, he's at the Briary,' Sarah said. Donna looked puzzled. 'The psychiatric unit at Harrogate District Hospital,' Sarah explained. 'I've been to see him a couple of times, and he's just . . . just *not there*.'

'What do you mean?'

'It's his body, but it's like no one's home.'

'So he won't be fit to stand trial,' Donna said.

Sarah broke into sobs and Mike comforted her.

'No,' Helen said. 'He doesn't even know his own name. There won't be a trial.'

'But he killed Charlie in front of everyone,' Donna said. 'Or rather, Reginald FitzUrse did.'

'He's lost his mind,' Ed said. 'He'll never get out of hospital.'

'I'm so sorry,' Donna said.

'So you bloody well should be,' Alec said. 'Selling crap like that spirit board, destroying people's lives. It's dangerous! *You're* dangerous.'

'Alec,' Helen said.

'No, he's right, Helen,' Donna said. 'Nothing like this has ever happened before. I've burned all my spirit boards and I know most other retailers have as well, despite the way people have reacted.'

'What do you mean, despite the way people have reacted? People have condemned them on the news.'

Donna shrugged. 'Hasn't stopped everybody wanting one. I could have sold a couple of hundred these last few days. People have come from Leeds, York and even further away to buy the exact same type that you used.'

The Castle Players stared at her, mouths open.

'Nowt so queer as folk.' Mike recovered first.

'I need a drink,' Helen said.

'I think we could all use one of those,' Donna said, smiling. 'The Borough Bailiff?'

'*No!* No,' Helen said, the second word calmer. 'I don't want to be in public, I can't face people, I'm sick of phones being stuck in my face to take pictures for their blogs and whatever. We can go to mine, it's on Finkle Street.'

The others nodded and, in silence, they crossed the Market Place and walked through the narrow alleys to Helen's.

'Wine, beer or gin,' Helen said, flicking lights on.

'Gin and tonic please – a strong one,' Mike said. 'Beer just won't do it tonight, and I never want to drink wine again.'

'I'll give you a hand,' Donna said, following Helen into the kitchen while the others found seats in the lounge and sat in a shocked silence.

Helen busied herself collecting glasses and ice cube trays. 'The gin's in that cupboard to the left,' she told Donna. 'And there should be tonic in the fridge.'

Donna opened cupboard doors, looking for the right one. 'Did you ever find the spirit board?'

'No. I don't know how many times we searched, but we covered every inch of that theatre and it was nowhere to be found.'

'Then how did it get into your kitchen cupboard?'

'What?' Helen turned and dropped the glass she was filling

with ice and lemon when she saw Donna holding the board. She pressed herself back against the counter, her face white with terror, arms stretched out as if to fend Donna and the board away.

'What happened, are you okay?' Alec said, rushing into the kitchen. 'I heard . . . Where the hell did you get that? How dare you bring another one of those things in here!'

'I didn't,' Donna said. 'It's the original one, I just found it.' She indicated the cupboard.

'Helen?' Alec said quietly. 'What's going on?'

Helen looked at him and her other friends gathered behind Alec in the doorway. 'I-I-I don't know. I don't know how that got there. Honestly, I don't.' Her gaze flicked between Donna and the others, eyes wide. 'You have to believe me, I didn't put it there.'

'You must have,' Sarah said. 'Who else would?'

Helen just stared at the lettered board.

'It will have been Broc,' Donna said.

'Broc? What are you talking about? We didn't call on Broc,' Ed said.

'Doesn't matter. He was connected to the others, they must have pulled him through with them.'

'Pulled him through?'

'From the spirit world,' Donna said. 'I suspect he's been with Helen from the beginning.'

'What about me? Does that mean a spirit's been with me too?' Alec asked.

'I think that's likely, otherwise you wouldn't have gone along with everything.'

'Mauclerk,' Helen said.

'How do you know?' Donna asked.

'It makes sense. Behind the scenes, though very much involved, and particularly close to Morville who was played by Ed, Alec's best friend.'

'I see,' Donna said, then paused as they all digested Helen's words. 'Well, that's not important now. We need to deal with this board, close it—'

'Destroy it,' Sarah said.

'Yes. Destroy it. Helen, Sarah, you finish off in here. The rest of you come with me to the garden, we need to make a fire. Do you have a barbecue stand or something, Helen?'

'Yes, in the shed.'

'Lighter fluid, matches?'

Helen nodded, pointing to one of the kitchen drawers.

Helen and Sarah, calmer now, joined the others in the garden, carrying six gin and tonics which they put on the table. 'Is it done?' Helen indicated the fire blazing in the barbecue.

'Not yet. I want all of you to do it,' Donna said. 'Mike, can you break it up somehow? Smaller pieces will burn better.'

Mike nodded, gingerly picking up the board, and he carried it to the back steps. Placing it down so it overhung, he stamped on it, splitting it, then again and again.

'That should do it, Mike,' Donna said, taking a gentle hold of his shoulder. 'Mike?'

He paused, took a deep breath, and nodded. They collected the splinters and handed them out round the group so each Castle Player had part of the board to throw on to the fire.

'Goodbye,' Donna said and indicated to the others they should say the same as they burned their pieces of wood.

'Goodbye, goodbye, goodbye, don't come back again. Goodbye you evil, murdering bastards,' Helen said, stopping only when Donna handed her a drink. She took a long, large gulp. 'Goodbye,' she whispered.

The others made similar sentiments as they threw the splinters of board on to the fire, 'Goodbye, good riddance, leave us alone. Piss off back to Hell.'

'Is that it, have they gone?' Ed said after they had watched the flames for a while.

'To be honest, I think they left in the theatre, once Henry and Becket had . . . ' Donna couldn't finish. She took a deep breath, then, 'This is just closing the door, to make sure they stay gone. Let's go in, though, and I'll double check.' She led the way, carrying her still full glass.

Inside she knelt before each actor in turn, closed her eyes a moment, then looked up at them from under her lashes. 'There's no one here that shouldn't be,' she said after a couple of minutes. 'Your auras are clear.'

'That's that then,' Alec said.

'Not quite. You've all been exposed to the spirit world, I want you to protect yourselves spiritually every day to make sure nothing else attaches to you.'

'You mean this could happen again? What, we're targets now?' Sarah asked. 'I've lost my husband, my children have lost their father, and two of the best people I know are dead, and this can happen *again*?'

'Possibly. Don't worry,' she added quickly, recognising panic in Sarah's rising voice, 'it's very unlikely, more to be safe than sorry really.'

'Too late for that,' Alec said.

Donna broke the ensuing silence. 'I want you to imagine wrapping yourselves up in a cloak of white light, so your whole body is covered, head to foot, can you do that now?'

Helen and Sarah nodded and closed their eyes, then the men agreed. 'Okay.'

'Now call on your guardian angels to protect you and keep you safe.'

Alec's eyes snapped open, then he closed them again – protest gone before it was uttered.

Donna waited a moment, then said, 'That's it, that's all you have to do, but do it every morning and every night. Make it part of your routine, when you brush your teeth, something like that, so you don't forget.'

'So what happens now?' Helen asked.

'Now you get on with your lives,' Donna said. 'As best you can.'

'How are we supposed do that?' Alec said.

'Well, Mike and I have been talking – I want to get away from this place, start again where nobody knows us,' Sarah said. 'Give John and Kate a chance at a normal life.'

'You'd take them away from Dan?' Ed said, incredulous. 'Hasn't he been through enough?'

'He doesn't even know who they are,' Sarah said. 'It nearly broke Kate when he looked through her and didn't recognise her. I know Dan's in hell, and I feel so sorry for him, but I won't consign our kids there too.'

'Well, you two bugger off then, take Dan's kids, *I'll* stick by him,' Ed said. 'I'll make sure he has someone fighting for him.'

'Yes, me too,' Alec said. 'We'll get him the best medical help, then the best legal help. He didn't do this, he was used by a vengeful ghost. It's not fair to just leave him in there.'

They sat in silence for a while, Sarah burying her face into Mike's shoulder, then Donna asked, 'What about you, Helen, do you have any plans?'

'I've had a lot of time to think about that,' she said and managed a small smile. 'I'm going to write a book about what happened.'

'What? Do you really think that's a good idea?' Sarah said. 'Surely it's better to try to forget, put it all behind you, not immerse yourself in it by writing about it.'

'How else will the real story be told? Everyone thinks that Paul, Charlie and Dan went mad – some kind of mass hysteria. As Ed just said, they weren't mad, and I want to set the record straight. I started all this by doing that bloody séance, I owe them that much, and maybe it will help Dan too – at least the proceeds may help pay for his care.'

'It's your penance,' Donna said quietly.

'Exactly. My penance.'

The End

If you enjoyed *Knight of Betrayal*, please consider leaving a rating and review on Amazon. Reviews and feedback are incredibly important to an author, as well as potential readers, and are very much appreciated.

For more information on the full range of Karen Perkins' fiction, including links for the main retailer sites and details of her current writing projects, please go to Karen's website:
www.karenperkinsauthor.com

Karen Perkins

Author's Note

Although a great deal is written about the assassination of Thomas Becket, barely anything is written about his murderers. Living close to Knaresborough Castle, where Morville, Brett, Tracy and FitzUrse fled and stayed in hiding after their crime, I wanted to explore these characters as well as the impact on their lives of what they had done.

It is debatable whether they were headstrong and bloodthirsty or truly carried out explicit orders of King Henry II, but the one thing the texts of the time do agree on is that Henry II carried out a public penance for his part in the murder of his old friend, the Archbishop of Canterbury, Thomas Becket in 1174. Not something that would come easily to a medieval king, I'm sure.

It appears to be true – and is certainly accepted fact – that his words, often misquoted as 'Who shall rid me of this troublesome priest?' instigated the vicious murder of Thomas Becket inside Canterbury Cathedral (this wording first appeared in Thomas Mortimer's *New History of England* in 1764, and the wording I have used in this book is inspired by the three contemporary accounts recorded by Guernes, Gervase of Canterbury and Edward Grim). Whether this was an order, a passing comment, or possibly a release of frustration by a man who, as king of England, was used to getting his own way – in everything – we'll probably never know.

There are very few accounts of the lives and deaths of the four knights other than the murder itself, and what does exist is conflicting to say the least. It is known, however, that after the murder, they fled to Knaresborough Castle and were shunned by nobles and peasants alike. The timeline of the knights' stay at Knaresborough is also unclear, and I have used the shorter option for purposes of dramatization.

There is also a suggestion that King Henry instructed them to go to Scotland, but as Henry was in France at the time of the murder and the knights appear to have set off north before he heard the news, I have 'reassigned' this advice as coming from Ranulf de Broc who, incidentally, appears to have suffered no consequences of his role in the murder. Henry II even granted him Haughley Castle a couple of years later.

The ends I assign to the four knights are what I think to be the most likely as they correlate to their family trees and the historical record – although as I mentioned above, many of the records are contradictory. Morville's children appear to have both been born after 1184, and Tracy apparently had two children in the 1150s, possibly another in 1170, although I have been unable to find a second source to confirm this, and two more in 1171, then another two in 1184 and 1185 with his second wife. Brett's first chronicled children are born after 1195. None of them had any children between 1172 and 1184, and I think this gives credence to the likelihood of an extended stay in piety in Jerusalem.

Morville and Brett left for their audience with the Pope and then the Holy Land months after Tracy's departure; but what prompted them to join him after all? Perhaps a king unable to regain the favour of the Church? A king – a medieval dictator – frustrated at losing his battle over clerical courts and blaming the knights who had brought about his fall from grace? A king who wanted to give his knights some 'motivation'?

There is no definitive record of FitzUrse after joining Henry in Ireland, merely a presumption that he either went with the others to the Holy Land or settled in Ireland. To my mind, this lack of information, coupled with Morville and Brett's decision to follow Tracy, suggests FitzUrse died in the Ireland campaign, but there is no historical source to confirm it, and his death as described here is fiction. Probably.

Whilst Knaresborough does hold an annual festival of entertainment and visual arts – feva – every year, the modern characters and personalities described in *Knight of Betrayal* are entirely fictional, including the members of The Castle Players, which is a fictional drama group. If you are visiting Knaresborough in August, I highly recommend the events that feva offer, there really is something for everyone.

Karen Perkins
North Yorkshire
21st March 2015

Acknowledgements

I am very grateful to the Dawn of Chivalry medieval re-enactment group, in particular Brian Robson. There are very few reliable reference sources for the 12th century, and without their help I would have found it even more difficult to make the details of this book historically accurate. Any mistakes on the historical detail (or anything else) are mine alone. If you ever get a chance to see Dawn of Chivalry in action, I encourage you to do so (website: www.dawnofchivalry.co.uk) The kids will love it (and so will the ladies . . .) For a sneak peek of one of their performances, see: https://www.youtube.com/watch?v=MVvd9lEDf6E

Thank you also to the Knaresborough Castle Museum, the Royal Armouries Museum Leeds, Royal Naval College Greenwich, Matt at the Coniston Hotel falconry centre, Janet Mitchell and the St Thomas a Becket Church in Hampsthwaite, and Practical Magick, all of whom have been very welcoming and helpful.

Thank you to the Knaresborough and Harrogate Writers' Groups, as well as the First Thursday book group, whose members have all been extremely generous in their advice and support, and have expertly steered me around many potential pitfalls – this is a better book for all of your input.

I have so much gratitude for my family: my parents, Russ and Helga; my sister, Christina, and my beautiful nieces Chloe, Natalie and Sophie (and no, you can't read my stories, girls, not until you're a lot older!).

Just as many thanks go to my friends, with a special mention to Louise Burke who bravely edits my books and doesn't flinch in telling me where I've gone wrong (she's usually right!), Cecelia Morgan, who never fails to design a stunning book cover, and Louise Turner who always tells me like it is. You have never wavered in your support of my writing, and I honestly could not do this without you.

I am extremely grateful for the support, advice, encouragement and opportunities given to me by other authors – whoever said writing was a lonely business could not have been more wrong. Especial thanks go to authors Elisabeth Storrs, Janice G. Ross and my fellow 'HotBoxers': David Leadbeater, Steven Bannister, John Paul Davis, Mike Wells, Andrew Lucas, CR Hiatt and C K Raggio. My journey so far would not have been nearly so exciting or fun without each and every one of you. *Thank you.*

Thank you also to Peter Illidge, Bernie Crosthwaite, who taught me so much, and Andrew Bennett and Peter Mutanda waNdebele who both encouraged me (in other words pushed me mercilessly) on to this wonderful and exciting path.

And most of all thank *you*, Reader. Without you, none of this means anything. I am humbled every time somebody reaches out to me either privately or in a review to tell me they've enjoyed one of my tales. I will do my best to continue to entertain and thrill you, and even give you nightmares – sorry!

Book Club Questions

1. Why do you think Morville, FitzUrse, Tracy and Brett were able to reach England so much quicker than the richer and more powerful knights Henry II officially tasked with arresting Becket?

2. What do you think was Ranulf de Broc's role in the murder: bystander or puppet master?

3. Why do you think Henry II placed no sanctions on the knights?

4. What role have few and uncertain sources, the language differences and superstition played on the recorded history of Thomas Becket's assassination? Can we be certain of the 'facts' of something that happened so long ago?

5. How important was the twelfth-century lack of any reliable, independent source of news in the canonisation of Thomas Becket?

6. Does Becket himself carry any of the blame for the events leading to his death?

7. How much responsibility does Henry II hold for Becket's murder?

8. In your opinion, has history treated the knights fairly?

9. Have you ever or would you ever experiment with a spirit board?

10. How much culpability does Helen carry for the modern-day killings?

Books by Karen Perkins

The Yorkshire Ghost Stories

Ghosts of Thores-Cross
The Haunting of Thores-Cross: A Yorkshire Ghost Story
Cursed: A Yorkshire Ghost Short Story
JENNET: now she wants the children

Ghosts of Haworth
Parliament of Rooks: Haunting Brontë Country

Ghosts of Knaresborough
Knight of Betrayal: A Medieval Haunting

To find out more about the full range of Yorkshire Ghost Stories,
including upcoming titles, please visit:
www.karenperkinsauthor.com/yorkshire-ghosts

* * *

The Great Northern Witch Hunts

Murder by Witchcraft: A Pendle Witch Short Story
Divided by Witchcraft: Inspired by the true story of the
Samlesbury Witches

To find out more about the full range of books in the Great
Northern Witch Hunts series, please visit:
www.karenperkinsauthor.com/pendle-witches

* * *

The Valkyrie Series
Historical Caribbean Nautical Adventure

Look Sharpe! (Book #1)
Ill Wind (Book #2)
Dead Reckoning (Book #3)

The Valkyrie Series: The First Fleet (Look Sharpe!, Ill Wind &
Dead Reckoning)

To find out more about the full range of books in the Valkyrie
Series, please visit:
www.karenperkinsauthor.com/valkyrie

About the Author

Karen Perkins is the author of the Yorkshire Ghost Stories, the Pendle Witch Short Stories and the Valkyrie Series of historical nautical fiction. All of her fiction has appeared at the top of bestseller lists on both sides of the Atlantic, including the top 21 in the UK Kindle Store in 2018.

Her first Yorkshire Ghost Story – THE HAUNTING OF THORES-CROSS – won the Silver Medal for European Fiction in the prestigious 2015 Independent Publisher Book Awards in New York, whilst her Valkyrie novel, DEAD RECKONING, was long-listed in the 2011 MSLEXIA novel competition.

Originally a financial advisor, a sailing injury left Karen with a chronic pain condition which she has been battling for over twenty five years (although she did take the European ladies title despite the injury!). Writing has given her a new lease of – and purpose to – life, and she is currently working on *A Question of Witchcraft* – a sequel to *Parliament of Rooks: Haunting Brontë Country,* as well as more Pendle Witch short stories.

To find out more about current writing projects as well as special offers and competitions, you are very welcome to join Karen in her Facebook group. This is an exclusive group where you can get the news first, as well as have access to early previews and chances to get your hands on new books before anyone else. Find us on Facebook at:

www.facebook.com/groups/karenperkinsbookgroup

See more about Karen Perkins, including contact details and sign up to her newsletter, on her website:
www.karenperkinsauthor.com

Karen is on Social Media:

Facebook:
www.facebook.com/karenperkinsauthor
www.facebook.com/Yorkshireghosts
www.facebook.com/groups/karenperkinsbookgroup

Twitter:
@LionheartG

Instagram:
@yorkshireghosts

Parliament of Rooks:
Haunting Brontë Country

by Karen Perkins
A Yorkshire Ghost Story

No matter how hard life is, humanity has the power to make it better – or even worse.

Parliament of Rooks, the new historical paranormal novel in the award-winning Yorkshire Ghosts series, contrasts the beautiful, inspiring village of Haworth today with the slum – or rookery – it was during the industrial revolution: rife with disease, heartache, poverty, and employing child slavery in the mills.

In 2017, life expectancy in the UK is 81.
In 1848 Haworth, it was 22.

Haunting Brontë Country

Nine-year-old Harry Sutcliff hates working at Rooks Mill and is forever in trouble for running away to the wide empty spaces of the moors – empty but for the song of the skylark, the antics of the rabbits, and the explorations of Emily Brontë. Bound together by their love of the moors, Emily and Harry develop a lasting friendship, but not everyone is happy about it – especially Martha, Harry's wife.

As Martha's jealous rages grow in ferocity, Harry does not realise the danger he is in. A hundred and fifty years later, this danger also threatens Verity and her new beau, William. Only time will tell if Verity and William have the strength to fight off the ghosts determined to shape their lives, or whether they will succumb to an age-old betrayal.

Read on for an excerpt from *Parliament of Rooks: Haunting Brontë Country* by Karen Perkins:

Prologue

Haworth, March 1838

Martha hitched up the bundle strapped to her front. Satisfied Baby John was secure, she grasped the handle and began to haul the full bucket up the well shaft.

John barely mewled in protest at the violent, rhythmic action, already used to the daily routine, and Martha pushed thoughts of the future out of her mind. Her firstborn was sickly, and she was surprised he had survived his first two months. He was unlikely to live much longer.

She stopped to rest, her body not yet fully recovered from the rigours of the birthing, then bent her back to her task once more. She had too much to do to indulge in a lengthy respite.

Once she had the water and had scrubbed their rooms clear of coal dust and soot, she'd be up to the weaver's gallery to start on the day's pieces.

She stopped again, took a couple of deep breaths, then coughed as fetid air filled her struggling lungs. Bracing herself, she continued her quest for water, cursing the dry February that had caused the well to run so low.

At last she could see the bucket, water slopping with each jerk of the rope. Reaching over, she grasped the handle and filled her ewers.

Adjusting Baby John once more, she bent, lifted, and embarked on the trudge homeward.

'Blasted slaughterman!' she cried, just catching herself as she slipped on the blood pouring down the alley past the King's Arms and on to Main Street. She'd forgotten it was market day tomorrow. The slaughterhouse was busy today.

Another deep breath, another cough, and Martha trudged on, the bottom of her skirts soaked in blood.

She heard the snort of the horses and the trundle of cart wheels on packed but sticky earth just in time, and was already jumping out of the way before the drayman's warning shout reached her.

'Damn and blast thee!' she screeched as she landed in the midden anext the King's Arms, which stank of rotten meat and offal from the slaughterhouse next door.

She clambered back to her feet, checked Baby John was unharmed, then noticed her empty ewers lying in the muck beside her.

Covered in blood and filth she ran after the dray, cursing at the top of her voice, then stopped. That wasn't the drayman sat atop his cart of barrels. It was a trap carrying a passenger.

She watched the carriage come to a halt by the church steps, and a jealous rage surged in the pit of her stomach as the passenger alighted.

Emily Brontë had returned to Haworth.

Parliament of Rooks: Haunting Brontë Country
is available now.

Bibliography for Knight of Betrayal

Barber R & Barker J (1989) *Tournaments Jousts, Chivalry and Pageants in the Middle Ages*, The Boydell Press, Suffolk

Barlow F (1995, 1999) *The Feudal Kingdom of England 1042-1216*, Addison Wesley Longman Limited, New York

BiblioLife, LLC *The Story of the English Towns Harrogate and Knaresborough by J.S. Fletcher*, BiblioLife, Charleston USA

University of Pennsylvania Press (2005) *A Knight's Own Book of Chivalry, Geoffroi de Charney,* Translated by Elspeth Kennedy, University of Pennsylvania Press, Philadelphia.

Corédon C (2004) *A Dictionary of Medieval Terms and Phrases*, D.S. Brewer, Cambridge

Guy J, (2012) *Thomas Becket,* Penguin Books, London

Hargrove E, *The History Of The Castle, Town, And Forest Of Knaresborough: With Harrogate, And Its Medicinal Waters.* Primary Source Edition.

Kellett A (2004, 2011) *A to Z of Knaresborough History*, Amberley Publishing, Stroud

Mortimer I (2008), *The Time Traveller's Guide to Medieval England*, Vintage Books, London

Domesday Book Yorkshire (Part Two), Phillimore, Chichester, UK

Thursfield S & Bean R (2001) The Medieval Tailor's Assistant, Ruth Bean Publishers, Bedford

Warren W.L. (1973, 1991), *Henry II*, Eyre Methuen Ltd, London

Secrets of the Castle (2015) BBC

Internet Sources

www.ancestry.co.uk

www.barhamhistory.com

www.devonguide.com/bovey-tracey

www.hampsthwaite.org.uk

www.knaresborough.co.uk

http://percyfamilyhistory.com/yorkx_files/yorkx.htm

www.stthomasabeckethampsthwaite.org.uk/history.html

www.yorkshireindexers.info/wiki/index.php?title=Hampsthwaite
_Parish_Church,_St._Thomas_a_Becket

Printed in Great Britain
by Amazon